The GLENELG
COUNTRY
SCHOOL

A
Margaret Wesley
BIRTHDAY
BOOK

· *presented in honor of* ·

memory of **Margaret Wesley**

· *given by* ·

Donald & Anne Bentley

D1596852

Remember Me to Lebanon

ARAB AMERICAN WRITING

Other titles in Arab American Writing

The Cairo House: A Novel
Semia Serageldin

A Community of Many Worlds: Arab Americans in New York City
The Museum of the City of New York

Hayati, My Life: A Novel
Miriam Cooke

Letters from Cairo
Pauline Kaldas

Post Gibran: Anthology of New Arab American Writing
Munir Akash and Khaled Mattawa, eds.

The Situe Stories
Frances Khirallah Noble

Remember Me to Lebanon

Stories of Lebanese Women in America

Evelyn Shakir

SYRACUSE UNIVERSITY PRESS

07   08   09   10   11   12   6   5   4   3   2   1

First Edition 2007

Earlier versions of some stories have previously been published: "The Story of Young Ali,"
Baltimore Review 10, no. 2 (Summer/Fall 2006): 39–46; "Oh, Lebanon," *Flyway* 7, no. 2–3
(Winter 2002): 26–33; "Remember Vaughn Monroe?" *Post Gibran: Anthology of New Arab
American Writing*, ed. Khaled Mattawa and Munir Akash, *Jusoor* 11–12 (1999); "Power Play,"
Knight Literary Journal 2 (2004): 142–52; "Name Calling" under the title "Any Other Name,"
Red Cedar Review 38 (2003): 35–44 and published by Michigan State University Press.
Permission to reprint these stories is gratefully acknowledged.

The paper used in this publication meets the minimum requirements of
American National Standard of Information Sciences—Permanence of
Paper of Printed Library Materials, ANSI Z39.48–1984∞™

For a listing of books published and distributed by Syracuse University Press,
visit our Web site at SyracuseUniversityPress.syr.edu.

ISBN-13: 978-0-8156-0881-3

ISBN-10: 0-8156-0881-0

Library of Congress Cataloging-in-Publication Data

Shakir, Evelyn, 1938–

Remember me to Lebanon : stories of Lebanese women in America / Evelyn Shakir.—1st ed.

p. cm.—(Arab American writing)

ISBN 0–8156–0881–0 (hardcover : alk. paper)

1. Lebanese American women—Fiction. 2. Lebanese Americans—Fiction. I. Title.

PS3619.H3532R46 2007

813'.6—dc22   2006035337

To George
who listened and read and encouraged

Evelyn Shakir, daughter of Lebanese immigrants to the United States, holds degrees from Wellesley College, Harvard University, and Boston University. A pioneer in the study of Arab American literature, she is the author of *Bint Arab: Arab and Arab American Women in the United States*, which will soon appear in an Arabic-language edition. As a senior Fulbright scholar, she has taught American literature to university students in both Lebanon and Syria; under the auspices of Bentley College (where she is professor emerita), she has taught similar courses in the kingdom of Bahrain.

Contents

Preface | ix

Acknowledgments | xi

The Story of Young Ali | 1

Oh, Lebanon | 17

Remember Vaughn Monroe? | 33

Power Play | 44

Name Calling | 57

Not Like Today | 69

The Trial | 89

House Calls | 105

I Got My Eye on You | 128

Let's Dance | 145

Preface

In 1876, the American centennial celebration brought a number of Arabic-speaking people to the United States. Merchants displayed their wares: icons, crosses, and rosaries from the Holy Land. Upon their return, word of their success spread and encouraged more travel and trade. International fairs in Chicago (1893) and St. Louis (1906) provided a similar impetus.

But already in the 1880s, not just merchants but wayfarers and immigrants were making their way to the United States. Those who came in the first wave, through the 1920s, were mostly Christian peasants from Mount Lebanon, which was then a part of the Turkish Ottoman Empire. These early immigrants peddled, worked in mills and factories, and became small-time (and occasionally big-time) entrepreneurs.

From the beginning, women played an active role as breadwinners, homemakers, and clubwomen. Sometimes they were trailblazers who adventured to America on their own or as advance agents for their families. After World War II, and especially after immigration policies were liberalized in the sixties, a second major wave of Arabic-speaking people came to America, this time from a wide range of Arab countries and at least as likely to be

Muslim as Christian. Though people of modest means and little education continue to be numbered among the newcomers, a significant segment are people from more privileged backgrounds, often students or professionals. Many, once again, have been Lebanese of different religious faiths, driven from home by the brutal civil war that raged from 1975 until 1990 and by the depressed economy that has yet to fully recover from the war years. Even today, people of Lebanese background constitute the largest segment of the Arab American community.

Acknowledgments

First thanks must go to Juliet Ayoob, her sisters, her cousins, her kin—women I knew in my childhood. They are the original inspiration for this collection of stories.

I am grateful also to Eugene Nassar, who encouraged their publication; to fiction writers Pierce Butler and Carol Magun, who advised on particular stories; to the anonymous "outside readers," who pointed the way to greater coherence and artistry; and to Mary Selden Evans, who has been the most gracious of editors.

Finding just the right photos for the collage on the cover proved challenging. For their help, my thanks to Pamela Yameen, Helen Samhan, Faten Freiha, Loai Naamani, Mohja Kahf, Richard Doughty, and Rouane Itani as well as to Devon Akman, Joan Mandell, Omar Al-Mahdi, Shihab Elborai, Hisham Kassab, and Pat Jaysane.

Several people kindly advised me on matters where my own knowledge was shaky—Joe Tamer (transliteration), Don Thomas (the geography of Los Angeles), Susan Holbert and Genevieve Fosa (Jewish conversion rituals), Vanessa Lane (teenage culture), and Kahlil Gibran (Boston's early Arab American neighborhood).

Maria Krings and Joan Oliveri helped me out in my battle with computers and printers. Philip Shakir inspired a story.

As it has in the past, the Virginia Center for the Creative Arts provided a precious opportunity for sustained writing.

Remember Me to Lebanon

The Story of Young Ali

When he's hurt my feelings or I'm in a mood, I try to spell things out for him the best I can.

"Number one," I say, "I'm not jealous of Cousin Leila's looks. But just for the record—you're a man, Baba, so I know you don't notice—I wear way less makeup than she does. Number two, you don't have to worry about me and boys and stuff, I'm not stupid. Number three, I do so remember my manners, and if I kept yawning when Auntie was talking, it wasn't my fault, I was sleepy."

"In the old country," he says, and tells me how it's cousin and cousin against the world, good girls don't hang out with boys, children pay attention.

Or else he pulls out this book. "Allow me, my daughter, to read you a story."

Which is exactly what happened on Thursday. Here's how that story began.

Sheikh Hamid, the elder of his tribe, and Ali, his sister's son, were riding home together once. To while away the long hours on horseback, Sheikh Hamid began to tell a tale. Ali was glad to listen, but his mind strayed for a moment when he saw something gold winking in the sand. He was cu-

rious but of course he would be shamed if he interrupted the Sheikh's narrative for a trinket of gold.

"You see?" said my mother. Actually, she said, *"Shifti?"* Mostly she talks to me in Arabic—so does my father—mostly I talk back in English. It was about an hour after supper. She was in the upholstered rocker, tatting more lace on top of the yards she'd already turned out. For my hope chest was the idea, which I didn't care about, but I did like to watch the shuttle dance in her hand.

"Listen and learn," my father said. He was in the wing chair with his legs crossed and his finger marking his place on the page.

I shifted around in the window seat and propped another cushion behind my back. "Next time I cross the desert," I said, "I'll be sure to remember."

My father wasn't amused. His breath whistled through his teeth. "If you please," he said to my mother, "why does this girl not know our ways?"

Her head came up, and her eyes opened wide. Blue eyes and her skin is fair, even though she's a hundred percent Lebanese.

"I do my best," she said, "according to my strength." Then she rolled her tatting into a ball, stuffed it in her apron pocket, and headed for the kitchen. At the door, she looked back. "The children belong to the father," she said. "He must answer for them before God." She swiped her hand toward the ceiling.

"So what happens next in the story?" I said just to defuse the tension. When my parents are mellow and okay with each other, they're beautiful to be around. He'll bring her a cup of coffee he's

---

*From "The Jewel in the Sand," in *Arab Folk Tales*, ed. Inea Bushnaq (Pantheon: New York, 1986).

brewed with cardamom and sweet the way she likes it. "Lady Miriam," he says, "may your days be like drops of honey" and offers it to her with a little bow. "Bless your hands, Wadie," she'll say.

Later on—if she's happy with him—she carries a basin of steaming water into the living room and sets it on a towel by my father's chair. After she pulls off his shoes and socks and rolls up his trouser cuffs, she goes back for a saucepan of cold and mixes it in until the temperature's just right. When my father's feet hit the water, he always says, *"Khayyy,* that feels so good!" Before the water cools, my mother massages his feet with her small white hands, one toe after another and slips her finger in between. She rubs the balls of his feet, his instep, his heel.

"*Ya,* honeybunch," she murmurs. That's a word she learned from reruns on American TV.

"Rima," my father said, "you ask what happens next?" He was fiddling with a rip in the book jacket. Bringing the edges together, trying to match up the pattern—zigzags and little diamonds and petals. We have an embroidered cushion on the floor with almost the same design, from Palestine or somewhere.

After a minute, he gave up. "Rima, your eyes are younger than mine."

"Tomorrow I'll scotch tape it for you, Baba," I said. "You won't even tell it was torn."

"God save your hands," he said and started in again to read.

So he let his lance—"that's Ali, you understand"—*he let his lance slip through his hand 'til its point touched the ground. As the two men rode on, it traced their path all the way to the camp.*

"He wasn't such a dummy after all," I said. "But still it wasn't a smart move because a sand storm could come up just like that and blow away the trail. He should have said, 'Excuse me a minute' to his uncle. 'I've got to check something out.' That's plain common sense."

"*Common sense*?" My father made a face like I'd put sour milk under his nose. "The sense of people with small minds, not heroes."

"Well," I said, not wanting to get sidetracked, "I still think the uncle would forgive him when he saw the gold."

My father took off his glasses and massaged his temples. "You don't understand," he said. "What are orange blossoms without their perfume? What is life without respect?"

"Mama, don't you think I'm right?" She'd come back from the kitchen with white paper napkins and a bowl of purple grapes. She set the bowl down by my father and handed him a napkin. "Try them," she said, "they taste of the old country." After she'd broken off a bunch for him, she held the bowl out to me. "*Tfaddali*," she said, "please help yourself. But no more arguing."

"This girl," my father said, and he began rolling up the sleeves of the plaid flannel shirt he wears around the house. "She listens but she doesn't comprehend."

Right then, I made up my mind. Let him read, I wouldn't say another word. But if I grew up with low self-esteem, which is one of the worst things that can happen to a person, he'd only have himself to blame.

The next part of the tale was about how Ali comes up with a cover story, says his wife should tell anyone who's looking for him that he's napping. Then he rides off the way he came, pockets the gold—it turns out to be a fancy piece of jewelry—and brings it back to the encampment. When his wife sees him, she says, *Sheikh Hamid has come twice to ask for you, and I told him you were sleeping.*

I couldn't believe what I was hearing. But I remembered I wasn't talking, so I just cleared my throat.

My father looked up. "You have a contribution to make, my dear Rima?"

"As a matter of fact, I do." I tucked my feet in under me on the window seat and pulled my skirt over my knees. "How come it's okay to lie to the uncle?"

"*Ya Allah*, what lie!"

"Wadie," my mother said, to remind him not to shout. She'd unrolled the last few inches of her tatting and was smoothing it out against the arm of her chair, admiring the pattern it made. My father lowered his voice and started asking me questions and then answering them himself. "Does Ali intend to deceive his uncle? No. Does he want to please him? Yes." His voice was getting louder. "The young man's heart is pure as spring water, his soul is white as the meat of a turnip. If you'd held your temper in hand, you would have heard that he carries the ornament straightaway to his uncle."

I rolled a grape around in my mouth and thought the situation over. "You mean like lying about a birthday party, so the birthday girl will be surprised?"

My father sighed. "All right, like a party." He turned to my mother and shook his head. She worked up that little smile, the one that says this is family conversation, nobody should get mad. Then my father leaned forward and looked at me over his reading glasses. He never finished high school, but when he stares me down like that with his dark round eyes, he reminds me of college professors in the movies. "My daughter," he said, making his voice sad. "You see the flea and not the camel. I begin to wonder, how do you get those A's in school?"

It was the perfect opening for my announcement. I sat up straight to make it. "I'm second in my class."

"Second?" my mother said. She stopped tatting and looked up. "That's very good. Did you hear, Wadie? Second."

"Are you sure, Rima?"

"Yeee!" My mother squeezed her eyes shut the way she does when her gout acts up or when she hears bad news again from home. "Have some faith in your own daughter. Of course, she's sure."

"It means I'll probably get a college scholarship."

"God is good," my mother said. "Tomorrow, Wadie, when your sister telephones, I'll tell her."

"I forbid it," my father said, and he was raising his voice again. "In this house, we do not boast."

"Well," I told him, "Auntie's always bragging about Cousin Leila. How she wears a size four and her hair is shiny as silk."

"Yes," my father shot back, "and what is more important, Leila is respectful. Do you think she debates her father as you do?"

Before I could think of a comeback, he sighed the way he does lately, pushed himself out of his chair, and said goodnight. I watched him climb the stairs, one hand heavy on the banister. Then I helped my mother pick up in the living room and put the leftover grapes back in the fridge. Sometimes we have our best conversations when we're working alone in the kitchen, but not that night. "I'm tired," my mother said after she rinsed out the bowl and dried it. "I'm going to shut the lights."

The next evening we were back in our same places. My mother tatting to fill her quota for the day, my father reading the newspaper and cursing politicians. I'd already mended the book jacket the best I could, and now I was on the window seat with my legs crossed under me, just watching the last of the sunset in the neighbors' windows. When the streetlights came on, I leaned back on my elbows.

"I've been thinking," I said. My mother glanced up. Her eyes drifted from me to my father, then back to her tatting. Her fingers had never stopped. My father folded the newspaper neatly and laid it on the table beside his chair.

"You make me happy when you use your brain," he said. "Tell me your thought."

I'd been planning how to put this to him.

"About the gold," I said.

"Yes, yes, the gold." I could see he was trying to encourage me. That's what's so great about my father. He blows off steam, but the next day he'll leave Hershey kisses on my dresser, or a little bag of roasted peanuts.

"In that story about Ali," I said, "*gold* doesn't just mean gold. It's a symbol. It stands for something else. For instance, being famous or anything a person sets their heart on."

That's what my English teacher calls an "insight." She's big on them, and I happen to have the knack.

My father rubbed his palms together. "Let us pursue this matter."

My mother was still tatting away, her fingers moving like a musician's. "Rima is right," she said.

My father put on this face like he was hurt. "Did you hear me say she was wrong?"

"And, Baba," I said—because I wasn't through—"the whole point of the story is to give up the thing you want."

My father took off his glasses and held them up to the light. Then he rubbed them against his shirtsleeve and put them on again. And all the time he was nodding at me and saying *yes, yes.* "You may recall," he said to my mother, "that my father's father, though he could not write his name, was known in our village and nearby as a philosopher. It seems this girl takes after him."

"Then you may set your heart at rest, she is your daughter and no one else's."

"For shame," my father said, but I could see he was trying not to laugh.

"Tell me, Rima." Just like my teachers, no matter how much good stuff you feed him, my father's always wanting more. "Why sacrifice what one desires?"

"That's a good question," I said and pinched my lower lip, the same way he does when he's thinking. "I guess because something else is more important."

My father's eyes were shining. "And this something else, what is it?"

I looked at my mother for a hint.

"Honor!" my father roared.

"Family," my mother said. Her hands grew quiet, and she looked hard at my father. "Who knows this better than you?"

"*Skiti!*"

Something in my chest turned over. I hate it when my father yells at her to be quiet, more even than if he lets me have it. I stared at my reflection in the window and the reflection of the lamp over my mother's head. After about a minute, I heard her say my name. When I looked, she picked up her tatting again and began telling me a story.

"In Lebanon," she said, "your father's people were not so poor and not so rich, somewhere in the middle. Most of the men worked a trade or ran a small business like a café or drove a taxi. Your father's father owned a pastry shop in our hometown of Bsharri, high up near the cedars. In the summer, the whole world came to Bsharri to enjoy the cool mountain breezes or, in the winter, to go skiing."

So far, I'd heard all this before.

"Foreigners came," my mother said. "From France, from Germany, from America." She took a quick look at my father, but he was staring into space. "Sooner or later," she said, "all the tourists would find your grandfather's shop because word circulated. His *ma'mul* and *ghraybi* were so delicious that if you tasted them, you'd be spoiled for any other. One customer was a man from Cleveland in America, and his wife. Middle-aged, I think. Anyway, not old. Every afternoon when school was out, your father waited on this couple when they came in for sweets and coffee. One day passed and then another. They noticed his good manners, they saw him reading at a table when he wasn't needed. How old were you then, Wadie?"

My father shrugged. "Fourteen years old," he said. Now he was staring down at the Turkish rug that's worn in spots but we still think it's beautiful.

"These good people offered him a gift you can't imagine. To pay for his schooling at the famous academy for boys in Suq al-Gharb and then at the American university in Beirut."

"But, Baba," I said, "you didn't go to college."

"No," my mother said, "because he was the younger brother and he thought the older, your Uncle Farid, should have the chance before him. But he never told Farid, he didn't want to shame him."

"I asked if they would bless my brother instead of me. They were very sorry, they cared nothing for Farid, they didn't know him."

"*Shifti?*" my mother said. "Your father sacrificed his education out of respect for his brother. This education was his gold, left buried in the desert."

"Baba," I said, "you made a big mistake."

His head jerked back.

"Rima!" my mother said, "is this how you talk?

He jumped up and started pacing. Snapping his fingers, and you could hear his breath each time he let it out. "Your fault," he said, standing over my mother. "I tell you no, but you must wag your tongue. And now here is your daughter, sitting on cushions like a sultan, wise enough to criticize her father."

That was yesterday. Today, Saturday, we all walked around on eggshells. I kept wishing I could take back what I'd said even though it didn't seem so awful. My father put on his oldest pants and spent hours in the garden, weeding my mother's flowerbeds and staking tomatoes. My mother drove to her sister's house. At supper, we were quiet.

But my parents can never stay mad for long. After I wiped the dishes tonight and stacked them in the cabinet, I stuck my head in the living room. They were going over house repairs that needed doing. My father was making a list on a pad of paper he keeps beside his chair. For a change of pace, my mother was crocheting. "But how many doilies will I ever need?" I always tell her. I don't want to hurt her feelings, so I don't mention they're out-of-date.

When my father saw me in the doorway, he waved his arm. "Come, sit!" Like I was company.

"Let's find out what happened to our friend Ali," he said and looked around for his book. I didn't want to break the peace, so I sat down and listened.

He picked up the story at the point where the sheikh is wondering who the ornament belongs to and figures it must be someone special. So he sends an old midwife to scout around the other tribes. Sure enough, she finds the beautiful girl who lost it, and she knows it's her because she's got another ornament that exactly matches. But instead of taking back the one she lost and saying thanks, the girl does something really cool. She says, *Grandmother, I want you to keep the jewel you brought me for all the trouble it caused you, and accept the other because they are a pair.*

My father looked up to see if I was paying attention.

"Awesome," I said.

"And would you be so noble, Rima?"

"The truth? I don't think so."

I guess he decided to look on the bright side. "At least she is honest."

"Rima is very generous," my mother said. "Last week she let her cousin Leila borrow her new jacket."

Anyway, when the sheikh hears what's happened, he decides he's got to have this fantastic girl, so he puts together a party of horsemen, takes Ali along, and heads for where the girl's tribe is hanging out.

At the camp with the many black tents, the men came running in welcome, bearing fodder for the horses, while the women spread out the mats on the guest tent floor. Whole sheep and young camels were butchered in plenty. When three days had been spent in feasts and banquets, the prince who was the girl's father asked the sheikh the purpose of his coming.

My father uncrossed his legs and laid the book face down on his lap. "We find here important lessons," he said, "precious guidance that we must not overlook." He held his fist up and unfolded one finger, then another and another. "One, two, three days must pass before you ask a man his business. Remember that."

"Three days," I said.

He held up two fingers on his other hand. "We Arabs are famous for our poetry"—he waggled one finger. "And our hospitality"—he waggled the other. "This is a case of hospitality." He was quiet for a minute, and I could see he was like my teachers, thinking how to drive the lesson home.

"Look at your mother!" That was so sudden, my mother jumped. "Does anyone enter this house, even a child, to whom she does not hasten to offer fruit or chocolates or cold juice from the refrigerator? Follow her example."

"Baba," I said, "I have friends, when I go pick them up, their mothers make me wait on the porch. And sometimes it's raining. Or if I get inside the house, they don't ask me even do I want a glass of water."

He looked at my mother. "Can this be true?"

She nodded.

"Americans!"

He sat there for another minute, making sucking noises with his tongue as if someone was jabbing him with a needle.

"Go on, Baba, how did the sheikh explain his business?"

Sheikh Hamid told the story of the jewel, ending with these words: "Then I began to feel a longing for its owner. And discovering that she is your child, I have ridden here to ask for her of you."

The father sighed. To ask is cheap and a daughter is dear. Yet how could he refuse a guest, one of such standing and send him away empty-handed? He said, "My daughter and my neck bow to you. Take her."

"Take her? Oh, Baba."

"Don't worry, Rima," my mother said. She knew where I was going. "Your father and I do not approve of matchmaking. I've told you so, many times. When you are old enough, choose a husband to please your taste. You will have our blessings."

My father was trying to get in a word. "Is that all you heard in what I read? Did you not hear the father's sorrow at parting with his daughter?"

His voice was gentle, and he smiled at me the way he used to when I was little and we didn't argue. I could feel my cheeks getting red.

"I heard," I said.

"Then let us continue the story," my mother said. I could see she was happy. Tonight she'd probably bring out the basin and massage my father's feet.

"Though, to speak honestly"—my father folded his arms and nodded his head at me—"we could choose better for you than you could yourself. Parents know which man will make their daughter happy."

"Perhaps," my mother said. "But all the same, Rima, you will dispose of yourself."

She started to get up and then sat down again. "Will this story of young Ali never end?"

"Reading dries the throat," my father said. "I have heard that homemade yogurt is the cure."

"Finish the story," my mother said, "and yogurt with fresh cucumber from the garden will be your reward."

The story seemed to be heading for a happy ending.

Sheikh Hamid returned to his people with a bride and a sumptuous camel train. A wedding tent was erected on the edge of the camp. The drums began to beat and the music to sound.

Then the sheikh called his nephew and said, "Ali, your bride is in the wedding tent, her eyes rimmed with kohl and waiting for her groom." "She is yours, uncle," said Ali. "You were the one to find her and to ask for her from her father." But the sheikh threw the fine wedding cloak over Ali's back and said, "The jewel was your find; none but you shall have her."

My father looked up at me and then at my mother. "Is it not a beautiful gesture?" He took off his glasses and dabbed at his eyes with a handkerchief.

"Baba," I whispered, "Ali already has a wife." He wasn't looking at me, and I wasn't sure he'd heard. I tried again. "Baba, they're handing the poor girl off like a baton."

He stood up, like he had all the time in the world, and walked around in a circle with his hands behind his back, the way my history teacher does when he's lecturing. Then he stopped and brought one arm down like a karate chop. "If," my father said, and he made it sound like a big word. "If a person takes pleasure in finding fault,"—he looked right at me—"she can always find something not to her liking. My daughter, do not reject the pot of rice because of one burned kernel."

"But he's a bigamist."

"Have it your own way, and let me finish with this cursed story."

He settled back into his chair, and then he coughed a little, and then he cleared his throat.

"I'll get you a glass of water, Baba."

"Sit still and listen," he said.

As Ali walked toward the wedding tent, a man threw himself on the ground and began to kiss Ali's feet. "Grant me the rights of a guest, Sheikh Hamid," he said, mistaking Ali for his uncle because of the wedding cloak. "Do not deny me, and may God brighten your destiny and good fortune bless your days." "Speak without fear," said Ali. "Then know that this girl is my cousin," said the youth. "We were promised for each other but her father, who is my uncle, could not shame you by a refusal when you came as a guest to his tent."

That was carrying hospitality too far, I thought, but no way was I going to interrupt again.

"You ask for what is yours by right," said Ali. He pulled the wedding cloak off his own shoulders and threw it onto those of the youth, saying, "May you find joy in your bride."

"And here is the moral," my father said. *So it is when men are noble!*

"The end," I said.

"Shifti?" my mother said. "You were ready to argue, but love won over all."

"Yeah, that part was cool," I said. "Baba, the story was kind of long, but, in the end, it wasn't bad."

"Thank you, my daughter," he said.

So I gave him a kiss good-night on the top of his head, where he's balding. "May your sleep be delicious," he said. I kissed my mother on one cheek and the other. "May you wake to happiness, my dearest," she said. I came to my room—that was maybe an hour and a half ago—and read a chapter of history homework just to stay ahead. Then I polished my fingernails, wrote in my diary, and climbed into bed. But now, instead of sleeping, I'm thinking about Leila. She lifts things from the mall. I told her once she'd better quit it or she'll land in jail. But it's just getting worse—Auntie can't figure out what happened to her gold hoop earrings. Leila's my cousin. I don't want to be the one to tell.

Which takes me back to the cousins in Ali's story and the way things worked out happy at the end. Come to think of it, though, I didn't actually hear the word "love." Maybe the boy just had first dibs on the girl, like the families had signed a contract or something.

I'll ask Baba tomorrow.

Oh, Lebanon

All her growing-up years, the family spent winters in Beirut, her father refusing—war or no war—to be driven from a city as much a part of him as his own breath. And, except for the year a militia camped in their country house, they still spent summers in the mountains. Like many well-off Muslims (and as long as roads were open), her father and stepmother sent their children to French nuns for schooling. She was the only one they sent to Anglicans. "On account of her English mother," they explained to friends, who got teary-eyed and murmured, "God rest her soul."

This school or that, to her it didn't matter. She moved stealthily through the days, from clearing to clearing, from terror to terror. "My father is brave," she thought. It was her comfort. He was also progressive and very rich. So when, at seventeen—ten years into the fighting—she showed him catalogues from American universities, he saw no problem. Felt, in fact, a tinge of pride. Just never noticed she was desperate to escape.

In her first semester at Wellesley, she met a junior at MIT, a black Jamaican with gentle ways, a hint of patois, and arched eyebrows like her father's. In all innocence, she wrote home about him. From that day, her father—not that progressive, after all—re-

17

fused her phone calls and burned her letters without opening them. The hurt she felt became defiance, then resignation. "He'll change his mind some day," she thought.

The summer after the Jamaican boy graduated, she visited him in Kingston. At first, she was tentative, but soon she fell in with the rhythms of the place—calypso, reggae, the spirit of his parents' teasing. When she held her own, giving back as good as she got, they were content, just as she was beguiled by green sea, lush hills, breezes perfumed with pimento and frangipani.

"Are you bored?" her boyfriend asked when three weeks had passed.

"You must be joking," she said and threw her arms around his neck. "I could live here forever."

As soon as she said it, she knew it wasn't true. Each day, news circulated of shoot-outs on the street and gangland executions; the murder rate, the papers said, was third highest in the world. When the mayhem got close to home, her boyfriend's brother-in-law stabbed outside his garden gate, the nightmares came back. Alone in bed, she tossed and dreamed of Beirut, rockets turning night to day, a teenage sniper ogling her from the roof across the street. Nearby, what had been an apartment building. Now just a grid of tattered cubicles, naked, taken by surprise. Then taken over—rats scurrying, squatters camping behind plastic sheeting, a militia-man stirring coffee over a coal brazier or hanging out wet skivvies. And yet you could emerge after laying low all morning in a shelter and know you were safe again 'til nightfall. In Kingston there was no moratorium.

"I can't live like this," she told him. He answered that away from Jamaica he would be a dull knife, an empty pod, a dry leaf. Cambridge had nearly sucked the marrow out of him, but at least he'd known it wouldn't last forever. He tried to blot out her fears with sex. Made love to her whenever they had the house to themselves. Even when she napped in his arms, he was whispering how he adored her golden skin, her green eyes; was bewitched by her breasts, her belly, and this, this! He ran his hand over the hot, wet place.

"I love you," she said. But that had nothing to do with it.

Back in Boston by way of Canada, she ran through a series of romances, some exhilarating to begin with, almost all of them short. The philosophy professor who dated his students on the sly—that had lasted a semester; the white-haired poet who wrote sonnets to his mother—he wasn't on the scene for long; neither was the pianist who cared for nothing but Chopin and Star Wars movies. Spells when she was on her own, she spent her evenings snacking on pistachios—she bought them by the sack, still in their shells—and reading expatriate memoirs. Most recently, she'd had a passionate fling with a Navajo mechanic who was so beautiful that every girl who brought her car in had made a play for him. He'd seen no harm in playing back.

Six months after their break-up she turned twenty-six, and depression took her by surprise. Her youth was gone, frittered away on men who had, each in his own way, been wrong for her. And what was to keep it from happening again since her own judgment had never yet guided her right? Now she understood why her uncle had arranged marriages for her cousins Mona and Aisha. It was an act of love. She used to be proud that her father was not old-fashioned, but now she was angry at his neglect. When she remembered how easily he'd released her to drift on her own across an ocean, she was astonished.

The fact was she'd been a babe in the woods here despite watching American movies all her life. "You have to be born to it," she thought. American girls were shrewd; they knew how to play the game. She'd been too needy. For the first time since she'd left Lebanon, she thought of returning, a college degree in her suitcase and no war now to scare her away. She took to dropping by a Palestinian grocery and stocking up on salted chickpeas, tins of halvah, and packages of frozen *mlukhiyyi* greens from Egypt. She found a Web site that posted Beiruti newspapers and read stories of warlords who were now government ministers. "I'll never go back," she swore. And, in the next breath, "It's too late anyway." In Lebanon she would be reduced to a dirty story, perhaps already had been. She was afraid her father would not let her enter his house.

"But what have I done?" she argued with him in her head.

"What will I do with my life?" she asked herself.

She'd been living on a combination of office temp jobs, gigs teaching Arabic calligraphy, and a bequest from her English grandmother. But that was no life. She could see now that Wellesley had been a mistake. History of art and Russian novels in translation when she should have been learning how to make money and cut a figure in the world. "We Lebanese are too sentimental," she told herself and signed up for an accounting class at the state university. After one hour with a guidance counselor, she was on her way. The woman had drawn a road map for her, checking off little boxes on a preprinted form. That sheet of paper set her mind at rest. Something tangible, something to explain why she was sitting in this classroom and not that one. "Next semester," she promised herself, "I'll enroll full time, and in two years or maybe less—if I go summers—I'll have my MBA." Now that she had a destination, she studied hard. True, the work was boring, but that's how she knew it would cure what ailed her.

One important matter settled, she turned her mind to the other. In bed at night, after masturbating, she thought about men and marriage. Back in Lebanon, her stepmother's housekeeper had taught her to snap the pointy tip of okra to test for freshness and sniff a honeydew for ripeness. But no heart-to-heart from anyone about sizing up a man. Not that she remembered. "Or did I just not listen?" What she needed was another sheet of paper with more little boxes to fill in. Another counselor who would study her like a book, then pull Mr. Right out of a database while she stood by, feet to the ground, hormones in check.

In the Sunday paper she found what she was looking for, on the same page as the personals. Curious, she skimmed them first. A divorced man was marketing himself as "a knight in shining armor seeking a damsel worth jousting for"; a widower was "a sea captain scanning the horizon for a mermaid."

"Oh, please," she thought.

When she met with the woman from the agency, she spelled out what she wanted—a sober assessment and rational match. "A man my family would approve of," she said and let it go at that. The agent pulled a six-page form out of her leather briefcase.

"I wish all our clients had your attitude."

The first man referred to her was described as three parts Lebanese, the great-grandson of immigrants from Tripoli in the north. She didn't know whether to be glad or sorry but thought, "I'll chance it." He turned out to be dark, slight, and with features that reminded her of her cousins. Thick hair, small ears that lay close to his head, a serious gaze. Altogether, more attractive than she'd allowed herself to hope for. He liked her looks, too—she'd seen his eyes light up when he first spotted her wearing the carnation they'd agreed upon.

On their first date, they met, as the agency advised, in a public place. From City Hall Plaza, they strolled to Quincy Market and found an ice-cream shop with tables outside, each shaded by a royal blue or tangerine umbrella.

"Let's go for blue," he said.

"Let's," she agreed, pleased that he noticed color although, truthfully, it was the tangerine that had caught her eye.

After ordering sundaes, strawberry for her, hot fudge for him, a full minute or more went by. She wanted to break the silence, to put them both at ease. But he seemed already at ease, one tanned arm thrown over the back of his chair, his gaze taking in the tourists and shoppers passing on the periphery of the café. She looked, too, trying to guess what he saw that prompted that look of contentment. The flow of colors and shapes, she thought; the balloons; the give and take of sunshine and shadow under the trees. Or maybe just his sense of being at home. It took an almost-Lebanese to remind her of her exile.

When she turned back, he was watching her, his arms crossed on the table. "You look happy," she said.

He smiled. "I'm happy you're Lebanese."

"What difference does that make?" The question came out more sharply than she'd intended.

"It makes a lot of difference," he said. "In my family, we've lost our Arab culture, and I'm the only one who cares."

"Poor you."

He laughed. "Poor them."

She liked it that he didn't take offense. Liked it, too, that he said "Arab." Some Christians in Lebanon—and he was Christian, she knew—refused that label. She was not a practicing Muslim. Even her father, for all his store of sayings from the Hadith, had never been devout. In fact, her own mother—his first wife—had been Christian. Still, she could never spend her life with someone who looked down on Islam or thought that "Arab" was a slur. She remembered a former boyfriend—the professor, it was—who had instructed her always to introduce herself as *Phoenician* or, if she must, as simply *Lebanese.* A warning finger raised. "Don't say *Arab.*" "Why not?" she'd asked. "It doesn't sound very nice," he had explained.

"Have you ever been to Lebanon?" she asked him. "Or to the Middle East?"

He shook his head. "No, I'm way overdue."

"Well, it's a distance."

"Sure, but you can bank on it—I'm going to get there soon."

Did he think she was his ticket?

She imagined returning to Beirut with a Lebanese American husband in tow. Imagined her father's pleasure because now she'd finally done it right. "You were sick with a fever," he would say, "but, praise Allah, you are well." He'd throw a party, the whole family would come, three generations of uncles and aunts and cousins. There would be long tables laden with food—everything from hummus and *baba ghannuj* to ice cream flavored with orchid extract, gum mastic, and rose water. She licked dreamily at the back of her spoon. The round of relatives (taking their cue from her father) would come up to her husband with an embrace and kiss him on both cheeks. They'd want to know in what town or village his family had its roots and inquire about his great grandmother's family name. "You are one of us," they would say, reclaiming her at the same time.

"Now *you* look happy," he said, calling her back to the present.

"Do you speak Arabic?"

"About three words. But I have this fantasy, I guess you'd call it." She waited to hear.

"It's set in the future. I'm walking down a street in Beirut. Name one."

"Hamra."

"Okay, I'm walking down Hamra Street with my son—let's say he's eight or nine. And we get lost. I'm assuming that could happen pretty easily."

"Probably not. Well, maybe."

"*Leave it to me, dad,*" my son says, and the little guy goes up to this man with a white beard and a fez—do they still wear them?"

"Not today."

"Okay, this man without a fez—and asks directions. In Arabic, you see, because my kid's been learning and he's fluent. The old gentleman invites us to go home with him to lunch. We meet his wife—she's a great cook, by the way—and his children and grandchildren. *My house is your house,* he says, and we become like part of the family. When my kid grows up, he marries the prettiest granddaughter."

She laughed. "And lives happily ever after."

"He's a good kid, he deserves it. But first,"—and he was laughing now, too—"I have to find a wife to teach my kids-to-be the *abc*'s of Arabic."

She looked past him at a cluster of tourists settled on a bench. One teenager in a Bruins T-shirt poked another playfully in the shoulder. Beside them, a young woman in a sundress lifted a plump little girl onto her lap and kissed the top of her head. Her own mother had died when she was three.

"Listen." He leaned forward, his small, shapely hands stretched toward hers. "Don't think I'm trying to rush things. I just want you to understand where I'm coming from, and"—he smiled wickedly—"I want to know all about you."

At first, they saw each other once a week, then twice or three times. They took in art galleries on Newbury Street, an afternoon concert at Mrs. Jack Gardner's Palace. One day he coaxed her onto a Duck Tour. They sat high in an amphibious vehicle that ferried tourists through the downtown streets. Pedestrians looked up and grinned. "Quack, quack," they teased. "Quack, quack," the tourists called back. "It's true," she thought, "Americans have no dignity." But he tugged her hair playfully and mouthed a silent *quack.* "Oh, why not?" she thought, and soon she was carrying on with the rest. When they rolled down the bank and splashed into the Charles, she caught her breath.

"Like it?" he asked.

"Wonderful!" she said.

Another day he led her through the South End neighborhood where the early Lebanese families—people like his ancestors— had moved in almost a century ago and then moved out in the for-ties and fifties to lose themselves in the suburbs. He stood with her in front of the townhouse that had once been home to the Lebanese Syrian Ladies' Aid Society, of which, he explained with pride, his great-grandmother had been a charter member.

She knew of Kahlil Gibran, of course? Knew his book *The Prophet*? She nodded. Well, when Gibran died, if she could believe it, he'd been waked in that very building, his remains brought up by train from New York for a funeral mass at the local Maronite church. Though one priest, hearing that Gibran had refused last rites, wanted to bar the door.

"When the funeral cortege went by, people all along here"— he pointed up and down the street as if he owned it—"they fell to their knees."

"How do you know these things?"

"I told you, I'm interested. I read, I talk to people."

Some time after the funeral—but this she already knew— Gibran's body had been shipped to Lebanon and carried high up the mountains for burial in his native village of Bsharri. Because that's the way he had wanted it. He'd wanted to go home.

"I know Bsharri," she announced. She had passed through it many times. To visit Gibran's grave? "No, not that," she said. But on her way to the ski resort higher than Bsharri, higher even than the cedars. Driving her Citroen along a narrow road, all hairpin turns and sheer drops down to ancient monasteries.

"Some day you'll show me," he said with such assurance that she could picture the two of them, hand in hand like children, exploring caves where Maronite Catholics had hidden for protection. Could feel his lean arm around her waist, in front of chains those same Catholics once used to restrain the mad and the possessed. On a damp September day in Boston, she leaned closer, then caught herself and stepped away.

By unspoken agreement, they avoided close quarters and stayed out of each other's apartments. Making a point of not getting physical, no more than an arm offered and taken, or triple kisses when they said hello or good-bye. Right cheek, left, right—Lebanese style.

Still, all the time now he was popping up in her thoughts. In bed, when she hugged her pillow to her chest and tried to remember the rough soft feel of his cheek; at school, breaking her concentration in the middle of statistics class or crisis management or macroeconomics. She'd be staring at a pie chart in a textbook, and suddenly there he was, darting across the page, happily dodging cars to come to her side of the street. If she fixed her gaze on the professor, she saw him instead. He was saying, "Yes?" and opening his eyes in surprise at something she'd told him, turning it over. In class sometimes she'd raise her hand to answer a question, but it was his approval that mattered. It warmed her to remember how she'd stumbled into it one day. "I think that's what I'd do," she'd said in an offhand way, and, without missing a beat, he'd declared, "Well sure, that's because you're a good person." She guessed he was the good person. If she fumbled in her purse for a tissue or a cough drop, she'd remember his wallet with his little brother's picture inside.

Three weeks into their courtship, he told her, "I feel comfortable with you." It was evening, for a change, and they were sitting at an outdoor café in Harvard Square. Dusty trees overhead, disreputable sparrows pecking at crumbs on the ground, in front of him a Sanka, in front of her an espresso, and between them, on a square of wax paper, the last of a corn muffin.

"It doesn't bother you my family is Muslim?"

"I love it your family is Muslim."

She forced a laugh, not knowing how to take that. "You love it? That's nice," she said, pouring more sugar into her coffee and stirring it slowly. "Mind telling me why?"

"Because it makes you that much more authentic. A card-carrying Arab. I want you to take me to a mosque, I want you to teach me."

"I don't think so."

He let it drop. "How about another round?"

"Sit still, I'll go." She knew he was watching her as she threaded her way among the tables and up to the counter. A breeze lifted her skirt, and she smiled.

"You have beautiful hair." She was unloading the tray. Suddenly bashful, she busied herself dealing out packets of sugar and plastic stirrers, then tossed her hair back as she slipped into her seat. It felt good to be with this person.

"What?" she asked, sensing that he was holding something back. "Go ahead, what?"

"Nothing. Just . . . well, let me put it this way. Did you ever think of wearing a scarf?"

It took her a minute to catch on that he meant a *hijab*.

"A rag on my head? No, thank you."

When she got home, she kicked off her shoes and paced from one small room to another. What a fool she'd been, and just when she thought she was growing smart. He was using her, like the others had, except for her sweet Jamaican boy, the only one who'd ever loved her, loved home more, though. Her mind was racing. The others, why had they wanted her? Not for herself, she decided, but smitten by some one thing about her, just as she might love the shimmer of silk in a certain light or the texture of a ripe avocado. She came to a halt in front of her bedroom mirror. No wonder those relationships had left so much of her beside the point. No wonder in the balance she'd been feather-light. But, oh—she started pacing again—Mr. Sheik-of-Araby was the worst. Trying to wrest her into something she wasn't.

"I was going to show up in a chador," she told him the next time they met. "I was going to walk into this café like a black shadow out of the desert."

A waitress in a striped jumper came by, and she asked please for iced coffee with milk.

He smiled at the waitress. "I'll have the same."

"Look," she said, "I think we're a mismatch. That's all I came to tell you. We look good on paper." She ran her forefinger across an imaginary page on the table. "But I'm not the woman you want."

"I think you are."

At an impasse, they waited until the waitress had set down their order. "Enjoy," she said and pulled out a pencil and pad, her eye already on another table.

"What can I do to change your mind?"

"Nothing," she was about to say but thought better of it.

"Tell me you'd hate me in a scarf."

"I'd hate you in a scarf."

"Don't say it like that,"—she rapped the table in irritation— "say it like you mean it."

"I do mean it," he said slowly, "scarf, no scarf, it's up to you."

For a minute, she watched him watching her. "You don't care about other men I've known."

"What counts is now," she heard him say. Well, of course, anyone could say that.

"You won't expect me to roll grape leaves or pickle turnips?"

"Did I ever say I did?" That sounded almost testy, she thought. Good. It wasn't natural—the way he was always brimming with good will. She remembered the mechanic. Never a harsh word, but that hadn't stopped him from cheating.

"Listen," she said though his eyes were still on her. "Don't think I'm going to recite the Koran five times a day. Or whisper Arabic in your ear at night." She tried to think of something else. "Or join the Ladies' Aid."

"I think the Ladies may be defunct by now."

She looked up sharply, but his face was sober. "Of course, I want children," she said, her tone softening. "But"—edgy again—"it doesn't follow that I have to tell them the folk tales my father told me about Jeha the fool, or teach them how to dance three kinds of dabka, or how to pickle eggplant stuffed with walnuts." She paused for breath.

"I can live with that." His tone was level.

"Because if there's one thing I'm not, it's pious. Or sentimental. I'm not going to fill the house with the music of Fairuz and Umm Kalthum."

"Understood," he said, but she was hardly listening.

"And you might as well know"—she rested her hand on her purse—"I don't carry around photos of our stone house in the village. And you won't hear me carrying on over the terraced garden that got blown up in the fighting or the olive trees uprooted, or the mulberry and quince." She felt tears rising and tried to blink them away. "Or my gorgeous cousin." She opened her purse and pulled out a tissue. "My cousin Fawzi. He got himself killed trying to cross the green line. And do you know why he was crossing?"

He shook his head.

"It was love. He had a girlfriend on the other side."

He drew in his breath, but she hadn't finished.

"If only I'd been in the city and not in the mountains that day." She swiped at her tears. "I'd have grabbed him by the arm and held on tight. I'd have said, *Listen to me.*"

He reached out his hand, but she shook her head. Then dabbed at her eyes with tissue, taking her time.

"Another thing." Her voice was almost steady.

He folded his arms. "Go ahead."

"This. I will not teach you Arabic."

"No? Well, if you can't, you can't."

The sun through the picture window was warm on her cheek. At the next table, two middle-aged women were giggling like girls. A young man with ruddy cheeks and toting a bike wheel walked through the door. She played with the straw in her glass, bending and unbending it, plunging it up and down, creating a sea of foam. Then looked up shyly.

"Your lies show you have a good heart," she said.

His face was serious. "You, too."

She looked around at the café curtains, the vintage pottery on display, the fancy breads on the counter. "This is a nice place."

He waited.

"Tell you what," she said with a smile. "No promises, but let's give this thing another chance."

He took a deep breath. "*Shookran*," he said in an absurd American accent.

She ran her hand through her hair. "You're most welcome, *habibi*."

"Now what's that again?"

"And you call yourself Arab! Don't you know anything? *Habibi*, my dear."

"*Habibi*," he echoed.

"No. If you mean me, it's *habibti* with a *t*. Because I'm a girl. Do you see?"

"I think so."

"Let me show you." She pulled a ballpoint pen out of her purse and began making squiggles on a paper napkin. Then shifted her chair closer to his and lifted his drink out of the way. "Now pay attention," she said, tapping his wrist. "Gender is easy."

Remember Vaughn Monroe?

Well, not to brag, but there was a time we used to be on speaking terms. It was after the war, when Vaughn had his own radio show and was hitting it big with numbers you never hear anymore, like "Racing with the Moon" or "Ghost Riders in the Sky." Nobody I knew of ever sang like Vaughn, in that deep voice, making you pay attention, just like he was somebody's papa.

The way I met Vaughn, I hired on to waitress at the Meadows. That was his own restaurant and lounge, right here in Framingham. Folks used to wonder "why Framingham?" The answer is Vaughn got his big break in these parts, and he was true blue—that's a well-known fact. The Meadows is long gone now, of course, but back then it was a pretty sight to see, sitting on a hill, lit up white like a Christmas tree, and a big neon sign flashing Vaughn's name down on Route 9. Not boasting exactly, just signaling folks: here's one of your own, made good.

As I remember, I went in at five to work my shift and, mind you, I got to dress up nice, with a black velvet band in my hair and another one 'round my throat. I even got to call Vaughn "Vaughn," right to his face, so that was something too. Right now I could show you a glass ashtray I saved with his name signed in purple, so deep it won't scratch out. You had to know Vaughn personally to get ahold of an ashtray like that.

Rubbing elbows with Vaughn got me to dreaming about show business and being like the next Rita Hayworth—except Rita was too beautiful—so maybe Ginger Rogers if I could save up money for dancing lessons and drop a dozen pounds. At home, I used to put a record on the Victrola and take a bow, like I had paying customers lined up on the sofa instead of just my sisters peeking in the parlor and laughing at me. But I didn't care. I just kept gliding and dipping and singing along with Vaughn's "Ballerina." That song, if you remember, was all about some gal who makes a big mistake 'cause she wants to dance on her toes and go 'round the world and be famous and have everyone love her instead of settling down with her boyfriend and being happy. You can learn a lot from a song.

Lucky for me and my dancing, our parlor was roomy. But the kitchen was close quarters. When I was in there, seemed I was always squeezing by somebody, b-hind to b-hind, or flattening one of my sisters against the icebox if they forgot and stepped in my way. Don't get me wrong, I wasn't ever what you call obese. But I am big boned. Plus, like I heard Mitch say, I'm well-endowed. He's my sister Emmie's husband and I remember one Thanksgiving, after a few beers, he's all over me in the two feet twixt the kitchen table and the sink. I don't go for that so I give him a good shove. "It don't bother me," Emmie says. Yeah, she's there too. She's laughing and Mitch is laughing. "Help yourself," she says to me, "I'd *like* a rest!"

Now, she didn't need to go and say that, hinting out loud about her and Mitch doing you-know-what. Suppose Papa walked in that minute to get himself a glass of water. Well, maybe he was gone to his reward by then, God rest his soul, but that don't change things—Emmie should of known better. We were brought up to know about right and wrong and "Shame, shame!" In gym class, I remember, we had to wear long pants 'cause the folks didn't want us in bloomers showing off our legs. Papa wrote a note to the principal to tell him, and I was the one had to carry it to the office. I cried and said I wouldn't, but Papa said I had to or he'd go in himself. And do you think we could stay after for Glee Club or even extra help? Or take in a Saturday matinee at the Rialto? Nope. It was go to school, do your homework, that's it. And, of course, *help out.*

Now I don't just mean darn Papa's socks and iron pillow-cases. I mean, *before breakfast* we'd be out weeding this humungous garden. Mama canned corn and beets and beans and peaches and pickles and grape leaves and three different kinds of jelly—and that's just to give you an idea. After the gardening, we'd wash the back stairs from up the attic bedroom right down to the cellar. *Plus* we all had to crochet for at least one whole complete hour a day. Don't ask me what we were making. I don't think it mattered one bit. Mama and Papa just figured we wouldn't get married if we couldn't crochet. Turned out, the joke was on them 'cause they had a hard time getting rid of us. We didn't know how to say cute things like American girls are always coming out with or how to do with your eyelashes to let a fellow know you could be interested.

With Emmie, it was easy. One day Mitch's grandma put her fur piece around her neck and rode the commuter cars from Boston to Framingham because she heard this family from

Zahle—that's her hometown in Lebanon—had a pack of "brides"—that's us—ripe for the picking. Mama made us parade from the kitchen into the living room, chests out, shoulders back, carrying trays of Turkish coffee and giant pistachios and home-made macaroons and Fannie Farmer chocolates. The old lady says, "Bless your hands" four times—to Evelyn and Yvonne and Antoinette and me—but when she sees Emmie bringing in the grapes, she says, "That's the one." Which didn't sit right with the rest of us because Emmie was only fifteen and had no business to be first.

But naturally we had no say. So Emmie got married and moved in with Mitch's family, old-country style. Then from morning 'til night, it's "Emmie, bring me a glass of water" and "Emmie, come brush my hair" and "Emmie, don't roll the grape leaves so tight." 'Til Emmie was mama to three sons—which made *her* somebody—and she began letting the in-laws get up and wait on themselves, and they began falling all over each other telling what a good cook she was.

After what Emmie went through, I let the world know I wouldn't stand for anyone pulling that "arranged" stuff on me, and so did my sisters. I guess they were waiting, like I was waiting, for a blue-eyed boy to romance me and promise to spend his life making sure I was happy. And it would be just between him and me and *no one* else. *American* style.

By the time I started at the Meadows, I was pushing thirty and figuring it's now or never. I shampooed my hair every morning and rinsed it with beer like the magazines say to; I plucked between my eyebrows—hairiness is the curse of our whole family, men and women, but it don't matter so much in a man. Last thing before I left the house, I patted bath oil that smelled like gardenia between my breasts. Dumb, when you think of it, because I didn't have the nerve to undo even the top button on my uniform. Anyway, mostly our customers came in couples, which didn't do me any good. Of course, sometimes when a guy's wife or girlfriend went to the ladies, he'd call me over and start in. "Hey, dark eyes"—stuff like that. But it wasn't my eyes he was looking at. I never could think what to say back or how to keep from breaking out in a sweat.

And all the time, Arthur was right under my nose, running the parking lot. The kind of boy you don't notice—he's got like no-color hair—but if you fall into conversation, you see he's got nice teeth and blue eyes. When he asked could he take me to see *The Treasure of Sierra Madre,* I said yes even though I never did like Bogie. He's too scruffy. I told Mama I was going with a girlfriend. By then, poor Papa had passed on.

Halfway through the movie, me waiting and still no girl, no romance, and Bogie going crazy, Arthur rests his arm behind me on the chair. I make out like I don't notice. Then his thumb, it felt like, was poking down and making circles 'round my shoulder blade. Do you think I dared move a muscle? Afterwards, he hardly said two words, and I was scared that I'd done something wrong. But I guess I passed muster because next Saturday he took me out again. We saw *Sorry Wrong Number,* with Barbara Stanwyck, who was never all that pretty, but she was smart. Except not in this movie. When the murderer got in the house, Arthur worked his hand in and squeezed my arm so I felt something happen in my breast, but I kept staring straight ahead. Then he leaned in like he was going to whisper something, but he just sort of breathed in my ear. I never knew what a little thing like that could do to a gal.

It was getting on in December, and I wanted to do things right. So I told Arthur to come by the house Christmas Day. I mentioned it to mama like it was no big deal. "You like him?" she said. But how can you talk to your mother about that? He showed up a half hour late with a fruitcake in a tin, which, as far as I'm concerned, he didn't have to. But it makes a good impression on the older folks. Even Emmie, who thinks she's something special, said what a beautiful tin it was. Arthur smiled a lot for about half an hour, so you couldn't help but like him, but then he said "sorry" and left before the refreshments came out, which we weren't expecting him to do. Still, in a way that was good. Mama put the fruitcake in the cupboard and we all stuffed ourselves with her homemade *baqlawa*—which is like Greek baklava without the honey—she made it better than anyone.

After Emmie and Mitch went home, I was in the kitchen with Mama. Just the two of us. Could be she told the others to steer clear.

"What is he?" she said.

"I told you, he takes care of parking at the Meadows."

"But what is he?"

So then I caught her drift. "Irish," I said.

She made that little sound she does with her tongue against her teeth. I knew what was going on. She was thinking that Italian or Greek, even Jewish, would leastways be a little better. Those people were like us, the old timers said. They loved their families and knew about honor. But the Irish were cold, like the English. Of course, first choice would be Lebanese, except from the day poor Papa came down with TB, no more folks from Zahle came calling to check us out. After he was gone, they still stayed away.

All in all, it turned out better than I expected. Mama said Arthur could visit if he didn't overdo it. But when I talked him into coming, she wouldn't let us walk downtown alone, and all we wanted was an ice cream soda. Evelyn and Antoinette had to tag along. After we turned the corner, he began cracking jokes. Said he wouldn't mind pretty chaperones every day. Said, "Anyone want to chaperone me home?" Still, no way out, he had to pay for all our ice creams. On the walk back, I slipped him a dollar bill, and he touched my backside, just for a second. That night in bed I touched myself there, but I couldn't get it to feel the same.

Then Mama turned against him. It was silly stuff. Like maybe she offers him chocolates and he takes a piece right away instead of hanging back. Or it got her goat how he's always waiting for *her* to say hello to *him* instead of him coming up to her first thing and asking how she's feeling. "Tell him not to come to this house," she says.

That's when I went back to sneaking. At almost thirty, a gal's got to think ahead.

Saturday was our day. I used to meet Arthur at Shopper's World, which was the first shopping mall in all New England and something for Framingham to be proud of. Of course, the thing *really* put Framingham on the map is these doctors who been testing the same folks for years, trying to find out what brings on heart trouble, but what do they know?

Our first date, we poked around in the stores, then we had apple pie and coffee at Woolworth's, and then we drove five minutes to Arthur's flat. I felt funny going, but he said, "Be a sport." He had four rooms upstairs in a two-family, and, for a boy, he kept it nice. First thing, he poured us out some wine—I didn't catch the name. All I remember is it was red and it made me cough. Arthur wasn't the type talked much. Just this or that about the Red Sox or about customers at the Meadows and their fancy cars. Mostly he let me gab. After a while, he said, "You're not like other girls," which I wasn't sure how to take. And then I let him kiss me, and that was all.

After that first time, we did the same—the stores, Woolworth's, and on to his place. His landlady would see us, and she'd wave. Which she wouldn't have if I was doing anything wrong. And then Arthur said he'd marry me. It was the sweetest day of my life so far. We stayed at his place 'til it got dark. When I got home, Mama was fit to be tied.

I was dying to tell someone. But who could I tell? My sisters were all thick as thieves with Mama. I did ask Emmie, did she believe in long engagements. She said, "No, why?"

"Me neither," I said. After that I started showing up early at the mall to look in Jordan's housewares department. I told Arthur about newfangled things—pressure cookers and steam irons— that we could buy or get someone to give us for a wedding present.

"Your mother's never going to like me." He started saying that.

"She will."

"Are you sure you want to go through with it?"

I got scared. "After everything?" I said, and I held on tight to his hand. "Don't worry about Mama, I'll take care of that."

"Just don't tell her yet, she'll spoil everything. Don't tell any-one."

So I didn't. But a person can't go on like that forever. It was too late for a June wedding, but the fall was nice.

"Arthur, what's wrong with October?"

We decided to elope. I can't remember which of us came up with the idea. Then I began turning over in my head the Arab girls I ever heard of that ran off to get married, beginning with old Mrs. Haddad's pretty daughter, Helen, the one who's a little slow. She went off with her second cousin. Then there's the youngest Khouri girl, her fellow was another Khouri, but no relation, and she told her mama ahead of time but not her papa. In our own family there was crazy Cousin Selma who fell in love with this pastry maker just off the boat from Damascus.

From what I understood, it always turns out the same. At first, the gal's folks cry and carry on like it's the end of the world, but sooner or later they say okay, it's the will of Allah and we have to accept it. What else can they do? They don't even know to think about annulment, and divorce is a no-no. And let's say the gal and fellow run off and forget to get married, that gal is damaged goods (even if she didn't do anything), so naturally no one else will take her. And the boy's folks have to go along, too, because it would be a big disgrace on them if their son don't stick to the girl now and be a good husband. So that was all right.

All through July and August we were spending time together, not just on Saturday but a couple of other days after work—we'd go to his place for an hour when the Meadows shut down at night. Sometimes I'd say no, I had to get right home because I didn't want Mama to start wondering, but Arthur would kiss my neck or brush the back of his hand across my breast, and that was that. He knew just how to treat a girl.

But, naturally, a person gets jittery when a wedding—especially if it's secret—is staring you in the face. Come September, we were both on edge. "Don't be so pushy," he said one day, and I began to cry.

The first week end in October, we made a date to get together to work things out. It's not like in the movies, with a ladder and a window, and a convertible waiting down the street. You've got to see about a license and find a justice of the peace and a place to stay and think about a little honeymoon, that was one thing I had to have. We met at his place. I took paper and a pen. We pulled chairs up to his kitchen table, and he said, "Let's talk."

So we talked and talked, and that's when I changed my mind. It came to me, clear as day, that I'm not the marrying kind. Well, Arthur's heart was broken, of course. He said he'd never cared for anyone the way he cared for me, and he never would. I told him, don't be silly. But he said even if he got married some day, he could never love her the same. And then he said something so sad. He said when he gets to be an old man and is dying and she's standing over him, he'll look up but he won't even see her and the last word on his lips will be my name. Wasn't that a beautiful thing to say?

Naturally, I felt sorry for him, but I'd made up my mind.

The next week, soon as I could, I took a bus up Maine to visit my Aunt Karimi and Uncle Latif. I wanted to get away so Arthur wouldn't be after me. A clean break is the kindest. When I got up there, what with everything that happened, I was feeling kind of sick. Uncle sent me to a lady doctor friend. She looked me over and said not to worry, that everything was all right.

When I got back to Framingham, I quit at the Meadows to make it easier on Arthur. And then—it didn't take me long—I landed a great job with the phone company. Long-distance operator, which was just right for me. I got to say hello to people in Europe and China. It wasn't like being Ginger Rogers, but it was almost good as traveling 'round the world. So I was happy and I've stayed that way.

Of course, I never married and neither did my sisters. When Emmie shakes her head at us and says, "I don't understand it," I say, "Never mind." What she doesn't know won't hurt her. If she goes too far, I might just say, "I've had my chances." I don't want her or anybody feeling sorry for me.

Power Play

Selma

Pieter was almost everything Selma could hope for in a son-in-law. He was clean, he didn't come to her for money, and, when she told about the old days, he listened and didn't tap his foot. His manners were beautiful, in the style of her overseas cousins, though he was Dutch, not Lebanese, and was born in this country. But, as she explained to her sister, old world in his bones. Eunice grimaced. "Like you, I suppose."

Other points in his favor: he took second helpings, he turned his hand to the little repairs around the house that had defeated her husband, and once he bought her a microwave. "Mind you," she told Eunice that time over lunch, "it's not even my birthday."

"Ha!" Eunice opened her eyes very wide, then went back to stirring her coffee. Selma didn't like that in her, the little sarcastic ways, especially with her being younger. But Eunice was right, there was a problem. After a year or two of Pieter being just what he should be, something in him went haywire.

"It's like you throw a switch," Selma told her sister one Saturday, "and the lights cut out."

Eunice found an apron and tied it around her waist. With nothing better to do, she'd answered Selma's call to help with spinach turnovers and meat pies for Sunday. While Selma pummeled the dough, Eunice peered into the icebox, then pulled out the washed spinach and scallions and reached for a knife. Soon flecks of green were littering the floor that had been swept just that morning.

Selma frowned and tried again. "It's like the tide's been coming in, and now it's going out. Or like when you're a kid and you hold a balloon tight by the string, but, first thing you know, it's floating away anyway, over the trees."

"Your son-in-law's nuts," Eunice said.

Selma gave the dough a final punch for good measure. "That's what I mean."

Lorraine

So far, it had happened three times. Lorraine would come home to an empty house and know, from the feel of it, that her husband hadn't just run out to fill up with gas or buy a tool from the hardware. This last time, she was out early from work and came in the back way. Pieter was still in the kitchen with his scuffed leather suitcase at his feet and a down jacket under his arm. She begged him, actually went down on her knees and clung to his legs. "Why are you doing this?" He disentangled himself and sidled past toward the door. When she heard the engine catch, she rushed to the window and banged on the pane. His ten-year-old Honda pulled out of the driveway.

Lorraine racked her brain. Last night, he'd been tender. Too tender. She should have guessed he was saying good-bye. It hurt her to think he'd caressed her and his curly head nuzzled her breast while that secret lay coiled in his brain. But maybe not, it could have been later, something that came to him in the night and confused him, a panicky dream or a voice. She should have watched over him, held him tighter. Or something at breakfast that ate at his nerves. Pits in the orange juice, eggs too runny, toast too light. Had she prattled on like a teenager? Sometimes she did that. She remembered him across the table that morning, his back to the window: the early light, like a halo, tinting his hair a strawberry blonde. But his face was a blur.

"You live with the man," her mother would say. "You must have seen something was wrong."

But nothing, she'd noticed nothing at all.

Selma and Lorraine

The drip, plop of the kitchen faucet was getting on her nerves. But what made her head pound, that was her daughter. Dumb, hopeless, bound to take Pieter back when he showed his face in a month or two. Oh, she might pout for a couple of hours, but sex—of course, that was it—would bring her around. She'd telephone Selma. "He missed me so much."

Selma tried to talk sense to her daughter, to appeal to her pride. "You're a wife, but you live half the time like a widow." Lorraine heard her out, then made her statement. She would not file for divorce, she would not change the locks, and she didn't give a shit what her mother would not have put up with. Selma couldn't believe it, the mouth on her daughter. But soon they were on good enough terms again and settled into the life they led when Pieter was AWOL.

Monday through Friday Lorraine went to her job in the court-house; evenings she did laundry, shampooed her hair, and paid bills or balanced her checkbook. On days she felt ambitious, she'd ride the exercise bike for thirty minutes while she watched *Wheel of Fortune.* She had a couple of friends from high school, married now, and once in a while, when one of them was home alone and bored, she'd dial Lorraine's number. At first, it gave her a lift to hear someone who wasn't her mother on the other end of the line. But the conversations were awkward, punctuated with long, breathing silences. After years of each going her own way, they'd lost track.

Selma kept busy as usual, vacuuming every day and scooting around—to doctors' appointments, to the Saharan bakery for bread and spices, to the butcher shop owned by an Armenian from Beirut. His was the only meat she trusted. At home, she sewed aprons and potholders to add to her stash. "You can never have too many," she told Lorraine. "I'm telling you so you'll remember."

Friday evenings now, she prepared dinner for two and had it on the table when Lorraine got off the bus at 6:45. Afterwards, in the den, they watched a video Lorraine had rented on her way from work. Anything with Doris Day or David Niven they both liked a lot. Saturday was free time. Lorraine could clean her apartment, shop for groceries, and mix enough tuna salad and boil enough eggs for five days of brown-bag lunches. Sunday after church, gas tank full, she and her mother visited great-aunts and cousins.

But Selma couldn't go long without stirring up the pot. "If I were you," she'd begin, and Lorraine would turn her face away.

Oh, if it were me, Selma thought, *I'd take him to court, I'd hire a private eye, I'd put his clothes out for the Salvation Army.* One Friday evening she tried a new tack. After toying with the last bite of custard pie on her plate, she pulled her chair in closer.

"I'm not saying *divorce,* but at least give him a scare."

"How do you mean?" Lorraine asked politely. Selma noticed her eying the clock. *As if what I'm saying has nothing to do with her,* Selma thought. *As if I'm reading from Dear Abby.*

Selma sat up straight. "Turn the tables."

"Like?"

"Like him coming home some fine day and you're not there." She stabbed the last of her pie and popped it into her mouth.

Lorraine pushed her own plate to the side; but, Selma noticed, she didn't get up.

"How would I do that?"

Selma had always had to think for her husband, too. If it weren't for her nudging—"You can do better, Charlie"—he'd have died driving a bus instead of fitting ladies in a shoe store.

"It's simple. When he decides to honor you with his presence, he always calls to say he's on his way. Am I right?"

Lorraine shrugged. "I guess."

"Of course, I'm right. He wants a hot meal when he walks in the door. Now here's what." She spoke slowly so Lorraine would see the beauty of her plan. "When the phone rings, don't you answer. From now on, let the machine pick up. If it's someone else, all fine and good, you can talk. But if it's him, you grab a nightie and head out."

"Yeah, well," her daughter said.

But it was an idea.

Eunice

Eunice had her own ideas. Pieter was a bigamist, plain and simple. Of course, the family couldn't see it. *Not my Pete,* Lorraine had said when Eunice dropped a hint. Selma turned it over, but, in the end, she said the same. *Your imagination's working overtime.* Her sister and her niece, two peas in a pod. One day Eunice had been at Selma's when Pieter dropped by to mount a shelf for her herbs and spices. After she set olives and cheese in front of him and poured him coffee, Selma had slipped upstairs to spritz herself with toilet water and smear on lipstick. *Don't you smell good,* Eunice announced, making a point of it, when Selma walked back in the kitchen.

Eunice admired Pieter's shenanigans. Not everyone could keep two sweethearts on a string, much less two wives. She still thought it was wives. One time, her tenth-grade chemistry teacher, Mr. Simms, gave her back a test with a C- on it. *I know you're smart,* he told her. *When you find what you love, you're going to shine.* Well, she loved making monkeys of the stupid boys she went to high school with, and later junior college. And she *was* good. Whatever fibs she told, they'd swallow whole. Especially Mike Snowe. After he saw her cuddling up to Danny Fedo in the caf, she said that Danny was her cousin and in urgent need of TLC. His father— Mike mustn't pass this on—worked for the CIA and was being held for ransom somewhere in the Middle East. When she touched Mike's cheek and rubbed her face against his sleeve, he bought it all. Anyone that dumb, she thought, shouldn't be allowed to cross the street without his mommy.

Not that Eunice didn't love her niece. She guessed she did.

Why else did she plan to leave Lorraine the pearl earrings and mink collar she'd inherited from her mother and a few thousand on top of that? Why else did she keep telling her, "Don't be such a sap"?

Lorraine

At first, she didn't remember and would reach for the phone. If it was her mother, there'd be a juicy suck of tongue against teeth. *Lorraine*, she'd hear, *you're not cooperating.*

The first time that she caught herself and listened for the message, she heard her Aunt Eunice on the phone.

"Pick up, I know you're there," Eunice demanded.

"Fuck you!"

Lorraine clapped her hand over her mouth. Where had that word come from?

Selma

There was a word for people like her sister Eunice. *Trouble.* Never happy unless she was making it for others or was in hot water herself. For instance, she was so pretty she could have had her pick of husbands, but she had to go for Elias Khouri. And for no other reason than he was the first guy who gave her a hard time instead of her doing it to him. Never mind he was a liar and a cheat, as Selma could have told her. In fact, did tell her. Maybe not in so many words, because Elias was Charlie's cousin and, in those early days, she didn't want it getting back to him. But she'd said enough. "Are you sure you know what you're doing?" And, another time, "Does this guy have a steady job?"

Selma had been in love with Charlie until she married him. Imagined all sorts of special things about him that turned out not to be there. She'd made the best of it. They'd only had the one child, and, of course, Charlie thought the sun rose and set on his little princess. Whatever she wanted—rocky road ice cream before dinner, the same Dr. Seuss three times over in one sitting, her best friend with them on a trip to Disneyworld—he couldn't tell her no. When she got to be a teenager, Selma set about to undo the damage. "Boys are tricky," she told her daughter. "Don't expect anyone to love you like your daddy." Lorraine had friends waiting for her at the mall. "I know all about it."

Lorraine was thirty-one now, and Selma had no grandchildren. That was the shame of it.

Selma took her coffee mug to the sink, washed and dried it by hand, and put it away on a shelf in the cabinet. She sponged off the counter though it didn't need it and stared at her reflection in the window. She remembered the first time Lorraine brought Pieter home for supper on a Saturday. Selma had cooked a meal good enough for Sunday, even made her special dessert, crepes stuffed with ricotta cheese and topped with orange-blossom syrup. "*Ahlan wa sahlan,* welcome!" She was all smiles as Lorraine steered him in the door. Oh, when Selma thought how good she'd been to Pieter, she could lay her head down on her arms and cry hot tears.

But that first visit, he'd made a good impression—white shirt and a tie, clean shaven, and with a shy laugh almost like a girl's. And a trade, refinishing furniture, that meant he could be his own boss or hire himself out, anywhere, anytime. Charlie had taken to Pieter in a big way. In bed that night, he'd touched Selma's shoulder. "Our little girl's got a boy top of the line."

Just the same, Selma recalled that she, for one, had always had her doubts.

"Don't say I didn't warn you," she told Lorraine when the troubles started.

"You didn't. You said he was Mr. Wonderful."

Her daughter could be stubborn.

On her way upstairs to run her evening bath, Selma hesitated in the foyer. She glanced at her watch, then picked up the phone, dialed, and listened for the beep. "It's me." She fluffed her hair in the mirror while she waited, but no one answered. "The only mother you'll ever have," she added and hung up.

Eunice

The morning she looked in the bathroom mirror and saw her swollen eye and the bruise on her chin, she decided it was over. Elias had run around on her from day one, he couldn't or wouldn't keep a job, and she knew he pilfered money from her purse. He'd even roughed her up before when he'd been drinking. Twisting her arm behind her back, dragging her to bed by her hair, tripping her so she fell hard against a table. For a month, two purple blossoms on her thigh refused to fade.

But so far it had all been private, husband and wife. This was different, an announcement to the world. Livid markings, like ugly graffiti, on her face. She paid Elias off, twenty thousand from her savings, and he flew back to Lebanon.

Eunice was propped up in bed, playing with the sash of her silk negligee and thinking of her sister. Selma had landed the good cousin, the made-in-America cousin. Eunice remembered the banners in her college dorm—"When better men are made, Pine Grove girls will make them." The first time Selma came down to visit, she thought the banners were advertising motherhood.

Eunice wanted to blame the old country for Elias's temper. But that wouldn't wash—her bashful father who marveled at spider webs and made pets of ladybugs had come from overseas. She held up two posters in her mind—Elias on the left, Charlie on the right and admitted that, even now and knowing what she knew, if she could pick, she'd choose the same. Elias had taught her that it took a bastard to make the blood pulse in her veins. Maybe for little Lorraine it was the same.

"I'll make her tell me." Eunice grabbed the portable phone from her nightstand and dared herself to do it. She was excited now, out of bed and pacing the corridor from bedroom to kitchen to living room. When the beep sounded, she announced herself and waited. "Oh, pick up," she whispered. Her face felt warm. Her heart was beating fast.

Lorraine

It reached the point, Lorraine flushed with pleasure to hear the jangle of the telephone. She'd hurry into the bedroom and wait while her outgoing message played, then lean closer so she wouldn't miss a word of what came in. After a while, no matter whose voice it was, she didn't answer.

She found herself keeping a list in a notebook by her bedside. Names, dates, times of day, and messages enclosed in quotation marks. Before going to sleep, she'd read through the list like a diary of her day. At first, if the caller left only a name and maybe a number or sometimes neither, Lorraine was disappointed. But soon the intervals of silence began teasing her imagination, like taunts from someone playing hard to get. She erased commands to "call as soon as you get home." She invented messages to herself and wrote them down. The good news wouldn't stop—bequests from distant cousins, a raise or a promotion, a boyfriend from junior high getting back in touch, a lady telling her she'd won first prize in the church raffle, an invitation to a party on a yacht.

Her few calls became fewer. Only her mother was persistent.

"Are you there, Lorraine?"

"Are you coming to supper, Lorraine?"

"Now, don't be silly, Lorraine. You pick up, I want you to pick up."

Lorraine would listen carefully to her mother's messages and sometimes she'd have to answer. Otherwise, Selma might show up in person, and she might bring Aunt Eunice or a policeman with her. "Hi, mom," she'd say, "I just walked in the door."

"Where have you been? What's keeping you so busy?"

Lorraine couldn't think how to answer.

"I saw the doctor, Lorraine. He says my sugar's up."

Lorraine gave a little "hmm" intended to show sympathy.

"A lot you care," her mother said.

Lorraine compromised. She allowed her mother one call a week and tried to drop by to see her for an hour on Saturday or

Sunday. Eunice she cut off cold. If you asked her why, she couldn't tell you. "Aren't you lonely?" her mother asked her. "It's not healthy to sit in that flat by yourself." She could kick herself she'd ever come up with that idea that started Lorraine not picking up the phone.

Eunice

Eunice changed her will. Lorraine out, Elias in.

Pieter

He felt strong. Like he could run uphill with a load of lumber in his arms. Like he could swim across a lake he knew in Pennsylvania. Like his heart would beat for days even if the rest of him were dead. And he was full of gratitude. For the trout in the lake in Pennsylvania and for wood fires at night. For farms with barns he'd slept in, for trails he'd hiked, for the girl with the red lips who laughed and tried to teach him Spanish, and for her brother who'd towed his car away when it died on the country road. Even for the waffles and bacon he'd had an hour ago in a diner this side of the state line. And now the breeze blowing through the window of the bus. He smiled at the passengers in the seats around him and noticed the girls. Not a one as pretty as his sweet Lorraine waiting for him at home. In the terminal, he hopped off the bus and headed for a phone.

Lorraine

When the phone rang, she had one foot out the door. She paused. No one had called in two days, and she was hungry for her fix. But then she changed her mind and turned the lock. This way she'd have something to look forward to all day. At the trolley stop, she was already imagining the wonderful surprise in store for her when she got home that evening. Composing in her mind the message that would make her the happiest girl in town.

Name Calling

"I got me the only rose on the family tree," Abe liked to say. When they were first married, Dolores took it as a compliment, and she'd color a bit, looking rosier than ever. But after a while, she caught on that Abe was boasting about himself, not her. And, more than anything, was being mean about her sisters. "The thorns," he called them.

When the children came along, Abe found a new twist on the joke. "Get ready, kids. Uncle Al and Thorn Lena are coming over— whatever you do, don't let her hug you!" Or—with a shake of the head—"Your Thorny Margaret, ain't she the sharp one!" Now that he'd got hold of it, he couldn't let it go. If one of his daughters answered back or made a face, he'd say, "Uh oh, looks like we got a little sticker pushing out here. Quick! Where's my scissors?"

"Papa's just teasing," Dolores told them, angry at him for getting them worked up, and angry at them for taking it to heart. "Barbara the barbarian," Abe would mock the older girl, his way to make her mind. She blamed her mother. Other mothers thought what they were doing, and named their daughters something pretty, like Rita or Marilyn or Amy. Finally, Barbara took things into her own hands and made everyone she could—not her father or teachers—call her Babs. The younger girl was Theresa. "Saint Theresa, cut that out!" Abe would yell although really she was the more obedient of the two. "We could call you Terry" was Babs's suggestion. But Theresa said no, that sounded like a boy's name.

Babs shrugged. "Suit yourself, Saint Theresa."

Dolores felt for her girls, but they'd get over it. It was herself made her feel sad.

"You should take a baking class," advised her sister Lena, drying dishes after Babs's sweet sixteen. "Learn to frost a wedding cake, there's money there. Or get yourself a job. Look at me, you never see me bored."

Dolores frowned. "Did I say I'm bored?"

"I've got a place where they're expecting me five days a week, rain or shine, cramps or no cramps. If I miss, the operation falls apart." Lena answered the phone at her husband's reupholstery shop and, between calls, reshelved the fabric books and vacuumed up the lint. "Things are changing," she explained. "Ladies can have careers."

Dolores couldn't think of a career and didn't want one, or any class either. She knew the name for what she wanted—*flower power*. She loved the sound of it. Once, at breakfast, she asked Abe, "What's this flower children business? Who gets to be one?" She was at his shoulder, pouring him his second cup of coffee.

Abe twisted around to look up at her. "You planning to apply? We got forms down the post office."

"That's not what I mean," Dolores said, turning her back to set the coffeepot on the stove.

"Better plan on dropping fifteen pounds. They got their standards, doll." He was laughing hard now, letting it out, choking almost on his toast and coffee.

"And don't call me *doll*," she muttered inside her head. On their first date ever, he'd called her Dolly, short for Dolores. "Please don't call me that," she'd asked him nicely.

"Why not?"

"I just don't care for it, is all."

He'd sighed. After that, he called her "doll." Which was worse, of course, but Dolores didn't have another protest in her. Didn't want him to be mad. Same thing their next date, when he unbuttoned her blouse and got his tongue in there. She kept her mouth shut, trying not to breathe in the pomade on his hair. Only gasped once when he pulled her on his lap and began bouncing her, slamming her into his crotch, fast and frantic, until—his fingers digging into her shoulders—he let out a howl. When he was through, Dolores didn't know what she was supposed to say or do.

Silly to bother about that now. She bought herself a spiral notebook with a paisley cover and started pasting in pictures from the papers and *Time* magazine. The first one, Abe himself came up with. "Here," he said, shoving the magazine under her nose, making a point. "See what the world's come to!" When he moved his thick forefinger off the page, she saw a girl, not much older than Babs, picnicking with her boyfriend. He was in shorts and bare to the waist. She was bare all the way but turned so you could just see the curve of her cheek, of one breast, the roundness of her ass up close. She was pretty all over. Like a healthy toddler, Dolores thought. Like her girls when they were babies, running into her arms, their cloth diapers bagging down to their knees.

Abe's thumb nailed the spot again, blotting out the girl's flesh. "If I ever thought one of my girls. . . !"

"They won't."

"If you brought them up right."

Later, with Abe gone to work, Dolores scissored the picture out and Scotch taped it to the first page in her notebook. After that, she kept the notebook hidden under half slips in the top drawer of her dresser. She'd pull it out, when no one was around, to add a picture or turn the pages. For a long time, her favorite was a black-and-white shot of soldiers standing at attention while girls in thin summer dresses stuffed daisies in the muzzles of their rifles. Dolores didn't follow politics, but one thing was sure—those girls weren't fraidy cats.

But it was the soldier boys her eyes kept traveling back to. Especially the smooth-cheeked youngster closest to the camera. There was something touched her about the way he stood so still, letting the girl in front of him have her way. Probably he felt foolish, but he wasn't going to yell or make a scene. He had his orders, Dolores guessed. But what if the girl stuck her tongue out at him, what if she slapped his face, what if she kissed him on the mouth? "He looks like a nice boy," Dolores thought. Her mind went to her Uncle Sammy who'd married late and had a child when he was fifty. He'd let that little girl do anything she pleased. One day, when Dolores and her mother dropped in, Sammy answered the door with metal curlers in his wispy hair. "We're playing beauty parlor," he said and gave Dolores a big, fat wink.

Much later, when Dolores was grown up and a mother, she'd let her own girls brush her hair, curling it over their little fingers or bobby pinning it into a sloppy French twist. Sometimes they'd top off the "do" with dandelions or stick buttercups behind her ears, then hold up a hand mirror so she could see. "Look how beautiful!"

"Just call me Dorothy Lamour," she'd agree, which made them giggle.

Underneath the photo with the soldiers, the caption said "flower power." The first time she'd ever heard of such a thing. After that, she saw it everywhere.

For instance, in this cartoon. A crowd of college kids in beads and smocks and jeans, parading down the street, looking happy and like they knew where they were going. But there was this cop in a phone booth. He was yelling, "Chief! They're armed with petunias, sweet william, marigolds, and roses!"

Dolores kept studying at the kids in the cartoon, then staring in the mirror. Until one day she stopped curling her hair. Abe knew something was different, but he couldn't put his finger on it. Of course, it didn't take Lena two minutes to spot the trouble.

"You're not letting yourself go to pot, I hope."

"I'm not letting myself do anything."

"You don't want to let yourself go."

Every afternoon now, before the kids came home, she took her notebook to the kitchen table and set herself to studying the pictures, the same way she used to go at algebra problems, trying to crack the secret of x and y. Or the way she used to stare at models in *Seventeen* and *Mademoiselle,* to find out how to turn herself American pretty. Her mother, who'd grown up in the old country, couldn't help her there, thought it was all nonsense anyway. "See how you worried for nothing," she said, when Abe from a good family back home popped the question.

After letting her hair go straight, the next thing Dolores did, she went downtown and bought herself a pair of sandals. Not the pretty white ones with dainty crisscross straps and skinny heels—two pair like that already sitting in her closet. But Jesus sandals, brown and flat, with sturdy soles that could stand up to rain and take a person any place they got a yen to go. Pretty soon, except for church on Sunday, she was wearing them all day and everywhere. Now she could take the dirt shortcut to the mailbox without twisting a heel, could cut across the damp lawn and not leave divots, could stand at the kitchen sink and wiggle her toes.

At the kitchen table, with her notebook open in front of her, Dolores was working on a list: "beads," "fishnet stockings," "tie-dyed shirt." She'd have to go gradual, so no one would notice. Like growing old, she thought. The folks who saw you every day didn't take it in, and then, before they knew it, you were dead. Except her plan was to go the opposite direction.

She was drawing a question mark next to "granny glasses" when Babs walked in on her. "Ma, I gotta get my ears pierced." Dolores flipped the notebook shut. "I'm the only one left in the whole class. I need ten bucks right now, they got a nurse at Woolworth's."

"You know what Papa said."

Babs didn't move.

"Okay, bring me my pocketbook."

It wasn't 'til later, with the lamb and okra simmering for supper, that Dolores remembered what Babs had ahead of her. If she knew her husband, he'd come to the table, take one gander, and bombs away! "You couldn't wait to cross me, could you?" Babs would sit there in a pout, her hands in her lap, and—if she knew what was good for her—not saying anything.

But that's not how it played. By six o'clock, Babs was in a mood, every few minutes waltzing into the kitchen and hugging her mother. When Abe walked in the door, she sashayed right up to him, couldn't wait to show off the evidence, tiny gold studs that had come home to roost. She lifted her curtain of hair with her arms, turned her head this way and that. "Papa, don't I look pretty?"

"Isn't one hole in your head enough?" he grumbled. And that was that. In bed that night, Dolores dreamed of young soldiers in granny glasses nibbling her ears.

The next morning she called Woolworth's, and the person who answered said, "Yup, 'til the end of the week." She grabbed her purse and headed out the door. "Might rain," she thought, but she didn't turn back or wait for the bus.

Block after block, she was remembering things. When she was a girl, you wouldn't think to pierce your ears, not if you lived to be a hundred. Once, though, a new girl, as dark as Dolores and with little gold rings in her ears, came into second grade. She could hardly speak English, and her name was too long and too hard to say. Mrs. Conlon led the little girl to the front of the room and turned her around to face the class. "I don't think our new friend will mind if we just call her Frances."

When Dolores reached Center Street, she slowed down, shifted her purse from one shoulder to the other, and came to a stop in front of a bakery. She stared at the cupcakes and cream pies and then her reflection, trying to picture that little girl's face.

"What you got on your ears, Frances?" At recess, a fresh boy in the class came up close and pointed. Frances stood very still, her face red, her dark brown eyes ready to cry. "What the heck are they?" He was showing off for the big kids. A fifth-grade girl shoved him out of the way. Then reached over and twisted Frances's ear lobes 'til tears leaked down her cheeks.

"Ugh!" the big girl said. "She's got nails in her ears!"

After that, only Mrs. Conlon and the principal called her Frances. In the schoolyard, she had a naughty new name. "Hey, Fannie," children would yell, running circles around her. "Hey, Fannie!" No matter which way she turned, they were tugging at their ear lobes and laughing their heads off.

At Woolworth's, the woman behind the counter said, "Make yourself comfortable, a couple young girls are ahead of you." Dolores sat on a stool by the jewelry case and leaned over to look at the studs. Tiny crosses, tiny pearl shapes, teensy daisies. "The smaller the better," she thought. The only jewelry her mother had ever worn was her wedding band. But in the old country a gypsy woman had come around each spring, with needle and thread, to pierce the ears of the little ones. "Did it hurt?" Dolores asked. Her mother couldn't remember.

Dolores had known other women from the village, some old enough to be her grandmothers. All dead now, her mother dead, too. When she was small, those old ladies gave her the creeps, and any time they dropped by to drink Turkish coffee with her mother or smoke a Philip Morris, she hid out in her room. But her mother always called her and made her kiss their damp cheeks and sit quiet while they gossiped in a hodgepodge of Arabic and English. "Don't let them talk to me," she'd pray. She couldn't bear to see the shiny vaccinations, big as silver dollars, on their arms; and their nylons rolled down to their ankles in summer; and the bedroom slippers they wore even to the supermarket; and especially their soft gray whiskers. Not to mention the holes in their ears. A long time ago, her mother's lobes had knit themselves closed. But these ladies must have been dumb as dishwater and put on heavy earrings every day. Dolores could tell because their ear lobes were droopy and yellowed, and showed gashes half an inch long. "You could hang a camel from," her father used to say.

"You won't feel a thing," the nurse said. She was standing at a little wooden table behind a curtain, and on the table was a towel and on the towel a metal contraption that reminded Dolores of pap smears. "Don't worry about a thing, sweetie. I do this every day and nobody's sued me yet." The nurse poured alcohol on a cotton ball and dabbed at Dolores's left earlobe.

"Tell me what you're going to do."

"Well, I make a mark here, just where the hole should be. And then I staple the stud in." She sounded matter-of-fact and cheerful.

"Make a mark?"

"Unless you'd like to do it, yourself, hon. Some people are very particular—they want it just so, not too high, not too low, not here, not there.

"Oh no, I trust you. Then what did you say is next?"

"The needle jabs right through here"—she kneaded one earlobe—"the soft, fleshy part. That's the trick, do you see? We don't want to run into cartilage."

"It's not a big hole, is it?"

"Oh, no, dear." She was brandishing the contraption. "That's a good girl, try to relax."

"Does it scar?"

"Shouldn't."

"You mean it could?"

"You're a worrier, aren't you, hon? You know we could have been done by now."

"I'm afraid I'm not very well," said Dolores. "If I'm better, I'll come back tomorrow."

"Whatever you say. But we got this far, it's a shame not to finish."

Riding home on the bus, Dolores was confused. Couldn't tell up from down, couldn't tell forwards from backwards. By the time she walked in the back door, she was feeling the way she used to after a killer math test, sure she'd got an F and scared what her parents would say. Of course, this wasn't the same. If she didn't want her ears pierced, if she'd thought better of it, that was nobody's business.

She dropped her purse on the kitchen table, then went into the living room and curled up on the sofa. She'd forgotten about Abe all day, but now she could hear him again in her head. From Day One of their marriage, he'd told her, "You're my wife. Be normal, you hear me? Don't call attention." And that's what she'd tried to do—what she'd always wanted even before Abe came along. When she was a kid, she hated being almost dark as a colored and having a mother who laughed too loud and sometimes spit right in the street, and old ladies around who didn't know the difference between slippers and shoes, and a father who reeked of cigars and tipped his hat to her girlfriends. Nobody else's father did that, not even to grown-up ladies. "Your father has a moustache," the lady at the candy store said to her one day. And then the woman laughed, her thin lips thick with lipstick.

Now out of the blue, after all those years of not calling attention, she'd gotten this idea. Wanted something those girls in the pictures had, though she didn't know how to name it. But she'd only been fooling herself. Because how could she be like those girls who knew where they were going and weren't under anyone's thumb? Forget they were so much younger and thinner and didn't have Abe to answer to, it was something went deeper. No old world in their head. "Maybe my girls can make it," she thought, "but not me."

"It's all for the best," she said finally, dragging herself up from the sofa and into the kitchen. Hungry for something sweet, she rummaged in the cupboard over the fridge. The bag she wanted was right where she'd stashed it, but ripped open and cleaned out, except for broken bits of chocolate and a heap of crumbs. "Those were *my* cookies." She shook the remains of the bag into her mouth. Her eye fell on a fresh jar of peanut butter, the girls' favorite brand that she'd bought them just yesterday. She unscrewed the lid and scooped out a fingerful, then stuck her finger in her mouth and sucked it clean. She experimented with forefinger, middle finger, ring finger, but her pinkie worked best. Scoop, suck, scoop, suck, 'til half the jar was gone and each breath she took tasted of peanuts.

Almost nauseous, she drew a glass of tap water to wash away the taste. Outside, the rain had arrived, a vicious downpour. Through the window over the sink, Dolores could just make out the shuddering clothesline and, in the border along the fence, the bowed heads of dahlias, mums, and late-summer roses. Could make out, too, where she'd gone wrong. Next time she'd print DO-LORES in big, red letters on a sheet of paper and attach the paper to the bag with an elastic band. Or with a darning needle. Or with her mother's six-inch hat pin.

Abe or the girls, it didn't matter. From now on, anyone poking where they didn't belong would be sorry.

Not Like Today

Fists stuffed in her apron pockets, Melia blocks the doorway. "I don't let strangers in the house," she says.

"Fine by me," I think. If we take off now, I'll still have time to hit the shoe sale at Filene's before the slingbacks that I like are gone. But no such luck, my mother doesn't budge, just stands there on the porch in a light cardigan that won't keep out the damp for long.

"I keep meaning to look in on you," she says. "But the car breaks down, or I have to stay home for the plumber. Last month I came down with the grippe."

Melia points with the little finger of one hand. "It's those thin shoes you wear." She steps aside and waves us in.

My mother's not like me. She swallows hard and does her duty, even when it comes to cranky in-laws. The worst of the crew are Melia and her sister Josie, my father's older cousins. Every six months, my mother makes a point of visiting them, writes it on her wall calendar in ballpoint so she won't forget. Like going to the dentist. But she's let it get away from her this year. Nine months have passed.

"Come with me, please," she begged.

"Only if we don't stay long."

She took that for a yes and phoned ahead.

In the kitchen, her back to the window, Josie hunches over the table. She's snipping flat round loaves of Syrian bread into quarters and then into eighths. When she sees us she narrows her eyes and stabs the air with her scissors. "Sit right there." No *hello,* no *how are you.* She must be saving up words in case either of us steps out of line. From the fridge, she pulls a platter and plants it on the table—sliced tomatoes, fresh mint, kalamata olives; and then a smaller plate layered with patties of white cheese.

"I hope you know I made that *jibin,* myself," Melia calls over. She's at the stove, her elbows hugging her sides, stirring the Turkish coffee with a long-handled teaspoon, letting the foam billow and subside three times before filling the tiny enameled cups.

The refreshments are predictable, and so is the conversation. Who's had another girl and still no sons, who's fading away to nothing from the cancer, who's running for president of the Ladies' Aid. While the three of them catch up, I nibble on Melia's cheese and think of other things. Whether to throw a party, why I'm cursed with hairy arms, whose fault it is if someone's husband makes a pass at me.

I'm working that one out when I realize that the room's gone quiet. When I look up, I see that Melia and Josie have me in their sights. Their eyes behind bifocals are ticking off the evidence against me: glossy lips, ironed hair, earrings dangling almost to my shoulders. *In for a penny, in for a pound* I think, so I shift my chair a few inches back and cross my legs. Now they have an unobstructed view—fishnet stockings, white thighs, under an orange minidress.

Josie's eyes are moist with indignation. She's never liked me. But it's Melia rises to the bait.

"Quite the up-to-date young lady, Miss Julia."

I smile.

"Out on your own now, I hear."

"It's the seventies," I say.

She captures a loose hairpin and jabs it into the thin bun at the back of her head. "Ah, Adele," she says, "the old days were best."

My mother nods. "The old days," she says.

"Have you told your daughter, Adele?" My mother looks up politely. "How our people came from across? First years it was hard times."

"Same for everyone, wasn't it?" I say. I uncross my legs and hook the strap of my purse over my shoulder, ready to leave. Why should I kowtow to these two old maids? But then my mother catches my eye. I know her creed: when elders speak, sit still and hold your tongue. Meanwhile Melia pits a black olive delicately with her fingers, then wraps olive, tomato, and mint in a piece of bread. An *'arus*, the Lebanese call that kind of sandwich. "Doesn't *'arus* mean bride?" I used to ask my mother. "Yes," she'd say as if it all made sense.

Melia brings the *'arus* halfway to her mouth, then returns it to her plate. "I don't blame you," she says to me. "What's family to you? I wish you'd been around when it was all we had to count on.

You know, Adele"—she's back at my mother again—"it's not right. The girl should know about her father's people so she'll be proud."

My mother is busy rolling her own *'arus* and licking her fingers. "You, Melia," she says, "you're the one knows your family best."

Melia smiles and now she bites into her bride.

She and Josie, they got their say, as usual, that afternoon. Melia in the starring role because she was older and entitled. Me, elbows on the table, waiting it out.

First, the story of their mother. I'd heard it so often, I could tell it myself. Left behind when her parents came to America to see about making money. After a year, the gifts began arriving. I knew the list—white kid gloves, then tortoiseshell combs, and then a steamship ticket: Beirut to Marseilles, Marseilles to New York City. The rest of the way, she came by rail. Word spread. (Here's the fairy-tale part.) The girl was "fair as the moon," she was "graceful as a gazelle." Her parents didn't like it, their daughter's name in every mouth.

"They married Mama off fast," said Melia. "To Papa because they knew his family back home."

"Just like that?"

"Yes, like that."

"Papa was a fine-looking man." Josie never missed a chance to set me straight.

Within a year, Melia was born, and then her sister, and so on. The fifth delivery brought pain, infection, fever. This time they took the mother to the hospital, where the nurses and her husband waited while she died.

"Mama was a saint," Melia said. "Ask anyone."

Then it was on to their father. After his wife was gone, he grew thin, began dragging his foot, gave up his customers—matrons he saw winters in Boston and summers on the Cape.

"Papa had real merchandise," Melia said. "Nothing dinky. Damask linens, crocheted tablecloths, silk negligees."

"I know," I said, to hurry the story along. "He was a peddler."

Josie rolled her eyes.

"Papa visited by appointment," Melia said. "Walked up to the front door like a gentleman, and the maid would show him in. *Be kind enough to step this way, Mr. Bourjaily.* The help was different in those days, such nice manners. And oh, the old Yankees, didn't they have class, didn't they have taste!"

"Not like today," Josie said.

"We were in a fix, poor Papa sitting at home and five mouths to feed. Who do you think saved the day?"

I played along. "Who?"

"Who else? Just fourteen and I got my first job sewing kimonos for Yusuf Aziz. That's before your time, Adele. He used to keep a few of us stitchers in the basement of his dry goods store."

"A harem," Josie said. I would have laughed if she didn't look so mad.

"I knew how to handle a machine. Mama had seen to that. I could ease the fabric under the needle, run a straight seam. And I was fast. Some of these women, they took all day to put a zipper in and still it came out puckered. I could do three for every one of theirs, and mine lay flat." She demonstrated with a paper napkin.

My mother nodded. "You have to have the knack."

"But you don't know what happened," Melia said. "When

Saturday came, Old Man Aziz walks in. You should have seen him. Three-piece suit he's wearing in July. *Gather round,* he says to us. Then he rubs his fingers. Abracadabra, he pulls an envelope from his jacket pocket, holds it up like this"—she fluttered her napkin—"gives it a shake, and out drops a wad of bills. The coins roll across the cutting table. *Just a young girl,* he says, *and new on the job.* He meant yours truly. I'd earned fourteen dollars and change."

"You were smarter than the others," my mother said.

"I was. And weren't their faces red. When Aziz left the floor, this piece of baggage from Damascus—Afifa was her name—lets fly with a wooden spool. Got me right here"—Melia touches her cheekbone—"almost knocked my eye out."

This was a new twist, and I guessed she was probably making it up on the spot. "A grown woman? She threw it at you on purpose?"

"If you must know, missy, she was sweet on the boss."

"Poor Afifa," I thought. I was sweet once on my poetry professor. And he led me on, he really did. Looked at me a certain way. Told me I was charming. And then he stopped. *You come across so high and mighty,* my girlfriend said. *So touch-me-not.*

"Why were you at work on a Saturday?" I said.

Josie answered. "In our day, a week's work was a week's work. We didn't cheat the boss."

My mother turned to me. "Half day on Saturday."

"And then we cleaned house when we got home," Melia said. "Papa would clear out, he couldn't stand the racket the Hoover made. He'd wash his face and comb his mustache and go."

"To the coffeehouse," Josie said.

"Oh!" My mother, brightened right up, the way she always did when the talk turned to the old neighborhood. "On the corner of Hudson and Oak? All our men went there."

"I went too," I reminded her. "*Jiddu* took me once, but you tried to stop him." *She's a girl,* my mother had protested. My grandfather pushed me out the door ahead of him. *She is child, no boy, no girl.*

So I could picture the scene, Melia's father sitting on a recycled kitchen chair, sipping *qahwi* with cardamom and smoking Egyptian cigarettes. He could be one of the men playing backgammon, who slung miniature dice across the board and snatched them up so fast I couldn't read them. Or one of the whist players who made me jump, the way they slapped down aces and trumps. Nickels and dimes passed from one man's stack to another. Low comments, too, that I couldn't make out.

"Papa heard things at the coffee house," said Melia.

"What kind of things?" I said.

"The kind we don't ever want to hear about you, Julia." She pushed herself up from the table—"Enough said"—and disappeared into the pantry.

What gossips the men were, I thought. The women, too, of course. I'd hardly met a Lebanese who didn't "move talk" or live in terror of the talk others moved. *What will people say?* I'd been hearing it all my life—when I was a kid and wanted to ride a bike or to stay out 'til dark watching the boys play baseball; or in high school when I wanted to spend the night at my girlfriend's, and my parents found out there were brothers in the house. Most of the time I got my way, but that didn't stop my father from sighing, or my mother from walking around with a worried look that took the bloom off my day.

In a minute, Melia was back, holding out a tray of sweets— sticky macaroons and bird's nest pastries stuffed with walnuts and lined in green with chopped pistachio.

"Oh, not for me," I said. She pushed my hand out of the way and slid one of each on my plate.

My mother served herself. "You're spoiling us," she said and took a bite. Then dabbed at her lips with a napkin and put back on her listening face.

"Papa would come home from the coffeehouse," Melia went on, "and he'd start in to curse Columbus."

"Christopher Columbus?" I giggled. "What did he have against Christopher Columbus?"

"You catch on slow," Josie said. "And you a college girl."

"He meant *America*," Melia said. "Papa blamed America. Back home daughters didn't dare do the things they get away with here. Remember, Josie? He used to tell us, *Better don't be born if you blacken my face.*"

"Was that some kind of threat?"

"You wouldn't understand," Melia said. "Papa was protecting us."

"He wanted us to be clean as snow," Josie said, "so no bastard could say a word against us."

"So he could hold his head up in the street," said Melia.

Josie looked out the window. It was November, bare branches and dead weeds. "You wouldn't understand," she said.

2

Melia scanned the table. "We forgot the fruit."

With a little groan, Josie got to her feet and opened the refrigerator. Apricots and grapes appeared on the counter.

"Wash them good."

I looked from one sister to the other. "I suppose you couldn't even date?"

"Date? No such thing," Josie said. She was running cold water from the tap.

Melia sat up straight and smoothed back her hair. "If I had my liberty, I could have stepped out every weekend. I'm not boasting. Did you every hear me boast? But I had plenty admirers, and all nice, respectable fellows." She turned to my mother. "I could tell you their names, Adele. You'd say wasn't I a fool to let them get away."

"Is that right?" my mother said.

For a minute there, my heart went out to Melia. Because I'd let a couple of good ones slip away, myself. One night, I met this perfect guy at a party, but when he called to ask me out, I made up some excuse. The truth was I couldn't picture us a couple—him so blond and fine featured, me dark, with fleshy lips and a wild bush of hair. I hadn't heard yet of *exotic*. When that came into fashion, I finally got an even break.

Melia glanced down at her hefty bosom. "You might not think it, but I used to be a tiny bit of a thing. I had a twenty-inch waist, I had a rope of hair thick as a fist. Do you remember, Josie? The high color in my cheeks. The landlady told Papa I rouged, but I never."

"You were the pretty one," Josie said.

"I was a looker, all right."

The late afternoon sun was in the sisters' eyes now. "Tell about the christening," Josie prompted and reached over to adjust the blinds.

"I had this Greek girlfriend," Melia began, "by the name of Alexandra. We were best friends. We covered for each other. This particular Sunday she took me to a home christening at her cousin's. I was in my prime, fifteen or sixteen."

"You weren't sneaking. Papa said you could go."

"But he never imagined. A roast pig in the bathtub and, in the kitchen, champagne corks a-popping. Oh, when I think of it! And on the back porch, astride the railing, riding it like a cowboy, a regular dreamboat."

My mother smiled. "He must have been family."

"The fellow had a friend. With Alexandra, that made enough for a double date, and we set something up. But Papa got whiff of it, and I couldn't go anywhere for two weeks, not even to Alexandra's."

"*Ooft,*" said my mother in sympathy.

"Yeah, too bad," I said.

"Dearie, you don't know. Even if a fellow in a fedora and tie knocked on our door, Papa would send him away. He'd tell him to his face, *You'll find no bride here.*"

"See?" My mother pressed my arm. "You see how it was?"

"I brought home the bacon," Melia explained. "I took care of the house. Without me, how would Papa manage?"

So we all thought about that, picking at purple grapes still wet with water from the sink, watching Melia stare into her coffee cup. Nothing but mud at the bottom.

After a bit, my mother coughed as if she'd had a thought. "Josie, you had a chance," she said.

Josie whipped her head around. "Who's been gossiping?"

"It's nothing," my mother said. "Don't upset yourself."

And then I remembered the story, how once Josie had been set to marry. Her aunt and his, neighbors in the old country, had made the match. A month before the wedding, Josie's father had broken it off. *How come?* I asked my mother one Saturday when we were cleaning house. She shrugged. *I wasn't on the scene then. But I heard the groom was seen walking on the Common with another girl, he had her on his arm. The family lost face.* She went back to dusting the venetian blinds. *Well, Josie should have eloped,* I said. My mother opened a window and gave her dust rag a good shake outside. *What are you talking about? Josie was ready to go after him with a butcher knife.* I stopped what I was doing. *That young man,* I said, *he was a lucky one.* My mother started to laugh, then caught herself. *Just vacuum,* she said.

"Lady of the house, that was me," Melia was saying. "I cooked, I cleaned, I did the laundry by hand. I looked out for the young ones."

"Little mother," Josie agreed.

"We didn't have luxury, just a few rooms, but it was warm, it was clean, it was home. Today you've mansions, but they're cold and there's no love inside. Each one shifts for themself, they're after the almighty dollar."

"Don't worry," Josie said—she was pouring more coffee— "God's keeping track." In the fading light, she spotted a smudge on the oilcloth and rubbed hard with her napkin.

"Adele." Melia reclaimed her attention. "Do you know how

much salary I kept for myself? Not a nickel. Every week, I'd hand my pay over to Papa. Right 'til the day they carried him out the door on a stretcher."

"What did he die of?"

Josie couldn't contain herself. "The hospital just as good as killed him."

"We should have kept him to home."

"If only." Josie rolled a grape around on her plate. Melia wiped her glasses on the bib of her apron. Then she picked up the thread of her story.

"Papa gave me change for the streetcars and a bit extra. I got along. But then Aziz started me stitching his samples and clerking upstairs, and I got a nice little raise. Of course, I didn't tell Papa because by then Grannie was after me."

"After you how?" I said.

"How do you think? She wanted a piece of the pie. And I was just a little girl, you might as well say. She put one over on me."

My mother wrinkled her brow. "Which grandmother was that?"

"Mama's mother," said Melia. "Her name was Saada, a little lady in black. You must remember her, Adele. She lived down the street from us at 15 Hudson. Sundays she smoked her *narghili* on the front stoop."

"15? Wasn't that the Syrian bakery?"

"Oh, much later it was the bakery! Don't you remember my *sittu*?"

"She cheated you out of your money?" I broke in.

"Not cheated," said Melia with irritation. "I didn't say 'cheated!'"

Backtracking. That was my mother's fault, with her questions.

"Granny *borrowed* money from my sister," Josie explained.

"No, Jo, she took it for safekeeping. She saw me pass on my way from work, and she called me to sit on the stoop beside her. *My heart,* she says to me, *why all wage they go to demon father?* She wanted to put some aside for me, you see. To look out for my future. So I let her have a bit every week, and she'd fold it away in her apron pocket."

Melia fell silent as if that was the end of the story. My mother reached for another pastry. Josie guided crumbs from the table into her hand.

"So *did* she save it for you," I said at last, "or did she spend it?"

"Of course, she didn't spend it," Melia snapped. "She slipped it to her son, my uncle, so he could treat his friends, be a big man. When the truth came out, there was holy hell to pay. Papa hollered and smacked me, and I cried my eyes out. Then he hustled over to Grannie's to get back his money, but no use, it was gone. *I never knew it was your daughter's,* Uncle told Papa. *How the devil should I know?* Well, Grannie couldn't let him get away with that. *You think dollar fall from fig tree into pocketbook?*"

"So she did sort of cheat you?"

"She did not! She thought by the time I needed it, she'd get it one way or t'other. Now don't say that she cheated me, Julia. That's not very nice." She turned back to my mother. "What's wrong with your daughter, Adele?"

"No, no." My mother set down her coffee cup. "Your *sittu* meant well."

"Grannie was very religious," Josie piped up, as if that settled the matter.

"Oh, she *was* pious," Melia agreed. "And strict as the pope.

Once she caught me sneaking back from the Denison House settlement. From a masquerade ball. I'd gone as a geisha girl, me and Alexandra went, she was a gypsy. We changed at her cousin's house, going and coming. I won first prize, I'll have you know, and they took my picture. I have it here somewhere."

Sneaking. I'd done some of that, myself. The few overnights I spent with a boyfriend, I needed a system even after I'd moved out of the house. First I'd phone my mother to tell her I was going to bed early so she wouldn't call and call and wonder. Next I'd make sure my sister had my boyfriend's number. In case of the disaster I was always expecting, someone would know where to reach me. In bed—before, during, and after—I'd wonder how long before I got caught.

"Did your father know where you were?" I asked Melia.

"Never!" she said. "Papa didn't believe in the social workers. He'd say, *Don't let the busybodies make fools of you. Are they your family to care about you?* And what made it worse, he was dead set against dancing. You know, we didn't dance two girls together, we danced a fellow and a girl. You did that, and the old timers thought you were headed for Hades."

That's when my mother spoke up. "They didn't know you have to keep up with the times. Even my brother Alec was like that. But my brother Khalil was different. He met his wife at a dance at the Denison. He used to go, and she used to go, and that's how they met. It was nothing shameful there. My father told us, *These women are trying to help our people.*"

Josie glared at her. "Well, weren't you the lucky ones?"

3

Melia was bending over the kitchen sink, rinsing her dentures. Then rinsing her mouth and spitting. "The nuts hurt my gums," she said. She wiped her lips on a hand towel and came back to the table.

"You were saying about your grandmother catching you?" I reminded her.

"Let me tell you," she said, lowering herself slowly into her chair. "To get from Alexandra's cousin's to home, the quickest way was by Grannie's. It was dark, about 10 o'clock of a summer night, and Grannie was on the stoop, getting a breath of air."

"I think I do remember her," my mother said. "And her husband. He was a big, strong man."

"Adele, he cried like a baby when my mother died. She was his pet."

"*Haram,* what a pity. And such a big, strong man."

"You know, Adele, he never wanted to come to America. It was Grannie. She told him she'd sell olivewood crosses door to door. Or she could tat lace and crochet potholders for him to hawk. Poor *Jiddu,* he wanted to stay snug at home, but she was jealous. She saw the neighbors gobbling up orchards and putting up houses."

"That's right," Josie said. "Laying out dollars from America."

"That's right," said Melia. "And Grannie wasn't one to sit with her hands in her lap while others got ahead."

"Well, why shouldn't a woman be ambitious?" I said. Melia and Josie paid no attention. My mother wouldn't look at me either.

"So there was Grannie on the stoop," Melia said, "and, of

course, she didn't like what she saw. Me out on the street alone at night. Next thing I know she's down the stairs and on top of me. She grabs my wrist, this one here"—Melia held up her right arm— "and twists it hard. *Naughty boy touch you, you let him?* she says. *You skin black tomorrow. The beoble, they see. You mother in heaven, she see.*"

"Mean old crow," I was thinking.

"I got away," Melia said. "I ran. But my wrist was hurting and, when I held it, that's when I felt my bracelet was gone. Adele, my heart was on fire. My mother, God give her peace, wore that bracelet on her wedding day."

"You don't mean you lost it?" My mother's hand went to her own *mabrumi*, one of those heavy bracelets of twisted gold the Lebanese pass down from mother to daughter. My mother's had a snake's head at one end, with tiny green stones for eyes. She used to rub the stones for good luck or when she was nervous.

"What I did," said Melia, "I turned myself 'round and ran back. And all the time, I'm praying, *Please let Grannie be in bed, please let me find Mama's bracelet.* When I got to Grannie's house, it was quiet as the grave." Melia lowered her voice to a whisper. "Dark, dark. I couldn't see much, so I went down on my knees and began raking the ground with my hand." Melia ran her fingertips over the tablecloth. "Next thing, I heard the door of the tenement open and then a step, too heavy for Grannie." Melia's fingers went still on the table. She cocked her head as if straining to hear.

"Guess who it was," Josie said.

"It was Uncle, out for a good time."

"Aah." My mother sounded relieved.

"He jumps a little when he sees me, but then he commences to whisper. *If it isn't my angel. What you doing there, girl? Stand up.* I couldn't help it, I started in to cry again. *Who's been mean to you?* he says and he steps on down to the pavement. *Tell Uncle, why are you bawling?* He took me by my elbows and lifted me right up. Sometimes you stand up too fast, you get dizzy, but he held me steady. *Don't cry,* he says."

"Uncles are always good," my mother said, "sometimes more than the fathers."

"He holds me tight, tight. Adele, what did girls know in those days? We knew nothing."

"Not like today," Josie snorted.

"Oh, today!"

"Adele, he starts licking my face like a dog. As God is my witness. Then he's at my mouth with his tongue. Here, here"—she pressed her lip hard with her finger—"he's pushing and not giving up. He forced me, and me just a little girl you might as well say." Her finger was in her mouth now, her lips moving wetly. I stared, and she slowly withdrew it.

"But I shouldn't speak of these things in front of your daughter, Adele."

My mother was staring, too, her eyes larger than I'd ever seen them.

I remembered one time with a boyfriend. I was flat on my back in bed, waiting, and he was kneeling over me. "I've got something just for you," he said. "Close your eyes and open your mouth." When I gagged and rolled away, he pinched my cheek hard.

"An angel in heaven must have been watching out for me,"

Melia said, "because I hear a voice—'Run! Run!' Uncle shoves me and I fall. But I get to my feet and I go like the wind. Just once I look back for a second, and what do I see? This black thing like a witch on uncle's back, it's Grannie pounding him with her fists. And him in a crouch, trying to pry her off, and, oh, the language out of his mouth."

"He was a devil," Josie hissed.

My mother, her face flushed, stared at her lap.

"All through history, men have . . ." I began, but Melia cut me off.

"Julia, who taught you, if you please, to ask so many questions?" She lowered her voice again to a whisper. "Adele, these girls today scare me. So bold, they live out on their own, home isn't good enough." She scraped back her chair and pulled up her housedress. "Hippies," she mocked. "Skirts up to here." She lifted her bum and hiked her dress higher.

My mother began buttoning her sweater. "Look how dark already," she said. She reached for her purse, jumped up, and moved toward the door. Josie was stacking dishes. I crumpled my napkin and handed over my plate.

"Good-bye," I said, scrambling after my mother.

"Ta-ta," Melia sang out and smoothed her skirt primly over her knees. But not before I'd seen the tops of her stockings and the hem of her corset cutting into her flesh.

Thirty years, but it stays with me, the kitchen, the pastries, the underwear. And my poor mother, gone now, my father gone, too. Melia and Josie, of course. I married a blond, an Irishman. It was either him or a Jew. Kev died two years ago, so I'm alone. My son's in California. My daughter's still in town, going to school for her master's, but last year she moved out of the dorm and in with her boyfriend. Wouldn't you know it, he's Jewish. "It's okay, Mom," she says, "he's not a Zionist." As if that's all I'm worried about. As if I shouldn't care my daughter's shacking up in clear daylight, and the neighbors with nothing better to do but look out their windows. In my day, we had the good taste to hide what we were up to. "Mom," my daughter says, and she gives me a hug. "You've got to keep up with the times."

Every two, three weeks, they invite me over for Sunday dinner. She's my daughter, so I go, and I'm nice to the boyfriend. Sometimes he calls me "Ma," just to be funny. One good thing, he loves our food, and once in a while I have them to the house and I cook. But they like it better if I just take them baked *kibbi* or stuffed grape leaves when I go on a Sunday. If they don't have it then, they'll eat it during the week.

Yesterday I carried over a sack with Syrian bread and black olives, and another sack with tomatoes and mint I picked fresh from my garden. My daughter unloaded my things and set them out in the pretty blue-and-white platters that she bought for herself. The boyfriend was tucking yellow cloth napkins under each plate. "Watch me," I said to him, and I rolled an *'arus*. Then I offered it to him like a little bouquet of flowers. "Bernie, can you guess what we call this?"

My daughter had to laugh. "Nice try, Mom," she said. Then she took my pretty *'arus* out of my hand, and brought it up to Bernie's mouth. "Close your eyes," she said, and I figured she's going to feed it to him like wedding cake, but all he got was a peck on the lips. Fresh thing, she wolfed it down, herself, then grinned at me like she'd done something smart.

I don't know. These days seems like I'm always figuring wrong.

The Trial

Like a lady with manners, the chimes sang out *good-bye, please come again* as Sadie opened the door and pulled it shut behind her. On the tiny stoop, she shifted her sack of groceries from one arm to the other, reaching down to be sure her change purse was back in her skirt pocket. Which reminded her of one last chocolate bar tucked away, she was almost sure, in the cookie jar on her kitchen counter. Now that she'd thought of it, she'd be disappointed not to find it there when she got home. Of course, there was nothing to stop her from stepping back inside and pointing to a Chunky bar with raisins or a Milky Way. She'd smile at Mrs. Kerner, a naughty smile that said, "I can't resist." Or smile a different smile and fib, "For my neighbor's daughter." Sadie shook her head at her own fool-ishness. "You'd think Mrs. Kerner was your mother."

From the stoop, Sadie could see in three directions. Up Pheasant, which was her way home, and west and east on Jefferson. The older she got, the more the avenue scraped at her nerves with its buses and autos rumbling in two directions. It didn't use to be so crazy busy, back when wooden streetcars rattled down an island in the middle and only families with money owned a car.

Sadie got a better grip on her groceries, but still the soft darkness held her on the stoop, like a friendly hand slipped inside her arm. This was what summer was about, she decided. Not sundrenched days, hot pavement, and noisy children leaping feet first into backyard pools, but this rich night smell of moist trees and earth silently composting; the chirp of crickets or drone of cicadas; ten o'clock, and the air still warm enough for an old lady to walk to the corner store and back without a sweater. She was sixty-nine, not even seventy. But last month she'd seen an item in the paper about an "elderly woman" in the South End, mugged on her doorstep. Sixty-five years old, the paper said. Since then, Sadie had been trying *old lady* on for size, thinking she'd better get used to it, seeing herself through others' eyes.

With one hand on the iron railing, she thought of the hill ahead, and sighed. Not a steep hill. Three years ago, she couldn't have told you, off the top of her head, if the road even sloped. But now, by the time she got home her right knee would ache and she'd be winded. Already she was regretting the weight of the half-gallon of chocolate milk and even the small jar of strawberry jam. After setting bread and paper towels down by the register, she'd eyed the other things and been tempted. She couldn't remember to think ahead. Just like a child.

Sadie took the rise at a steady pace, peering down at the asphalt sidewalk, watching her step. After a block, she decided, not for the first time, to get herself one of those carriages on wheels to roll behind her to the grocery. Farther along on Pheasant lived nuns who ran a day-care center, and she noticed that's what they used when they went shopping. And they were young. These were vintage nuns with long black habits to their ankles, except white now in summer. Sadie wasn't Catholic, so probably not entitled to a vote, but she didn't like the way most nuns today looked like civilians. Modern, she supposed, but boring. Half-hearted, when you came to it, that's what it was.

Halfway home, Sadie lowered her bag onto the hood of Mr. Foster's Honda and paused to catch her breath. In front of her was his wife's flower garden. Year after year, her blossoms were the glory of the street, color lapping on color, petals preening in the sunlight. But Sadie almost preferred the flowers at night, the way they stood around in closed committee, their gaudiness sloughed off. Ghostly hollyhocks in charge of the agenda, mums plump as matrons—she thought of the Khayal twins who showed up at meetings of the Ladies' Aid dressed in tight bodices that showed their cleavage. Dead-headed peonies like dumb Evie Tawa, who never got the point. Pansies were junior members of the club—how well she knew their type—bunched in a corner, silly creatures making foolish talk. But she'd better cut that out, the way her imagination ran away with her. "You do know none of this is true?" her niece had said one day when Sadie reported on a spat between her dishwasher and her electric teakettle.

Sadie had just retrieved her groceries when she spotted a fig-ure ahead bearing down on her. Fear stirred in her throat until she saw it was a woman. Sadie could make out her shapeless dress like a tent, billowing to one side and then the other. The scuffs on her feet clopped fast and noisy against the pavement; a purse, the shape of a saddlebag, slapped against her side. In one fist, she clutched a limp plastic sack. As she came on hard, the woman had the air of someone who'd given up minding if people stared or else just knew they would, no matter what. It was the size of her. Huge all over—face, frame, and a bust that seemed to demand wide berth. What must it be like, Sadie wondered, to push that prow through space, it always arriving a step before the rest of you. Like an impatient companion pulling ahead.

Only a few yards away now, and the woman showed no signs of swerving. At the last minute, Sadie ducked. But instead of racing by, the woman pulled up short, grabbed Sadie's arm for balance and then, in a rapid role reversal, steadied Sadie so she didn't fall.

"You're all right, I've ahold of you," she got out, still breathing hard. Sadie was too indignant to speak, then too indignant not to.

"You nearly knocked me down!"

"Boo hoo"—the woman thrust out her lower lip—"aren't you the crybaby." She gave Sadie's arm a shake before releasing it. "Buck up, I've told you that a hundred times."

Sadie was flabbergasted. "But I don't know you."

The woman stared off to one side as if trying to remember. "Well, never mind"—she smiled brightly—"friends again."

Sadie hugged her bundle closer and stepped aside, a hint for the stranger to be on her way. But whatever sense of urgency had been driving her seemed forgotten. As if she'd come across something more important to attend to, she was studying Sadie's face by the sallow light of a nearby street lamp. Sadie stared back, taking in the bulbous nose, the baggy eyelids, the flowered muumuu, its colors muddy in the lamplight, her lips off-color too, thickly smeared with lipstick. Her age was hard to figure. Fifty, maybe fifty-five, though she'd been moving like a younger woman. But what did it matter? Sadie longed to be in her own kitchen, putting her few groceries away; then curling up in the corner of the sofa with a bowl of butter pecan ice cream; leafing through the half-price catalogue that had come that day in the mail. No one to tend to but herself since her mother had died, no one to answer to.

"Good night," she said and took a step.

"Inti bint 'arab?"

Sadie turned her head, wondering if she'd heard right.

The woman repeated herself, lining up the syllables. *In-ti— bint 'a-rab?* As if speaking to the slow witted or to a child.

Sadie nodded. "I'm Lebanese," she conceded. She could have answered in Arabic; she knew enough of her parents' language for that kind of simple give and take. But she felt intruded on by this stranger, and speaking to her in Arabic would have established an intimacy she didn't want to offer.

"Ana kaman bint 'arab," the woman announced.

Well, that didn't come as news. If she was speaking Arabic, of course she was Arab, too. And, from her accent, also Lebanese. But there it was, in the assertion, in the small lick of the lips, in the satisfied tone—assumptions being made, claims being laid. And, eager as she was to get away, Sadie didn't have the heart to flout a lifetime's training and turn her back. Her parents, to their credit, had never pressured her to love Lebanon, a land she'd never seen. It was enough for them she'd been a good girl and learned from them what mattered. Hospitality, family before self, respect for elders. Chastity went without saying. If her mother were alive and here instead of Sadie, she'd be thrilled to meet, in this unlikely way, someone who spoke her language. Assumption for assumption, she'd be of one mind with this woman, acknowledge kinship, lose no time finding out who her family were and from what mountain village. Track to ground, if possible, a common blood relation. To all these matters Sadie was indifferent. She lacked that something remembered in the genes: one clan against another, strength in numbers.

While Sadie mused, the woman shifted her weight, letting her shoulder bag slide to the sidewalk. Then she spoke up again.

"You know the Haddads." It was part question, part assertion. As it happened, Sadie knew probably a dozen Haddads. In Arabic, a name common as Smith. In fact, in Arabic a name that meant smith. Sadie paused, poised to go either way.

"Retta and Emile," the woman continued, gesturing with one finger over her shoulder. Sadie peered obediently into the dark. But it was no use playing dumb because, of course, she knew Emile Haddad and his wife. They lived in a brick Tudor on a street that crossed Pheasant, no more than a five-minute walk from this very spot.

"Their grandparents were friends with my mother and father," Sadie admitted. Best friends, she might have added and kind to Sadie from the time she was a little girl. Khalil Haddad, gone more than a decade now, used to trot her around on his shoulders while she clutched his shirt collar. It was almost her earliest memory. From kitchen to hallway to living room, in and out doorways. "More," she'd say, "more." And always cheering them on from the sidelines dear Auntie Matile, who'd lasted maybe two years after Uncle died of a heart attack.

"My cousins," the woman announced with a note of triumph.

"Your cousins." Sadie produced a smile and set down her bag, propping it against the Fosters' fence. Now there could be no question of rushing off.

For the first time that evening, Sadie felt a chill. The breeze was picking up, and she could hear leaves chattering in a maple overhead. She glanced up. On the largest bough, hidden in its busy shadows, she caught glimpses of unusual activity, two figures swinging their legs like children. It was Uncle nodding at her and smiling, his gold tooth catching the light. And Auntie blowing kisses that settled on Sadie's cheeks like moths. Both of them, she immediately knew, trusting her to do right.

"Your cousins!" Sadie repeated. "Oh, but I haven't seem them in ages." She pitched her tone carefully. The words beneath her words were meant to say, "To my regret, to my loss, and nothing could please me more than spending a day with them—please God, tomorrow."

"Nobody home," the woman announced as if answering a question.

For a minute, Sadie thought the woman meant her. She remembered her father teasing her when she was a child, tapping her forehead with two knuckles.

"I rang, I knocked. Believe you me, I made a ruckus."

"What a shame." Sadie had caught up with the woman's meaning. "Didn't they know you were coming?"

"What am I supposed to do now?" the woman wailed. Embarrassed, Sadie cast a look around. The woman's voice was loud. It would draw the neighbors to their open windows. It might scare off spirits lingering in the trees. Sadie glanced upward, but it was hard to see.

The woman poked Sadie's arm. "Listen, I took the train from Fall River to Boston and hopped a bus out here. That's half a day wasted. And now I've missed my connection back." She put one fist on a hip and scowled. "I hope to heaven you stopped me for a reason."

That was so outrageous, Sadie couldn't let it pass. "I didn't stop you at all."

"You just as good as did. Standing there like a traffic cop."

"That's enough," Sadie thought. She hardened her heart, picked up her bundle, and started walking.

"Don't be that way," the woman called, coming after her. "Don't you see? I thought you were Retta on your way home."

Sadie turned to face her. "Me?"

"Of course, when I got a good look, I knew it couldn't be, you're too old. You can maybe fool me from a distance but not face to face." She shook her finger coyly. "You little dickens." Then she reached out and pinched Sadie's cheek.

Sadie pulled away. "Stop that!" she cried.

"You always were touchy," the woman said with an exaggerated sigh.

"Tell me," Sadie pleaded. "Am I supposed to know you?"

"If I can just make it to South Station.

"Yes," Sadie said, "that's what you need to do."

"But"—the woman repeated her point—"I've missed the last bus that can get me there to catch the train home."

"Maybe not. If I were you, I'd run."

"No," the woman said in such a mournful tone that Sadie thought she might cry. "It's too late." She cupped her hands as if testing for rain. "You see how it is." Her arms collapsed to her sides.

It's not your problem, Sadie told herself, but how did that change things? It didn't make her go away, this strange creature who'd been full of beans two minutes ago but now seemed to be shriveling before Sadie's eyes. Sadie mustered her most cheerful tone. "You can call a taxi."

The woman lifted her head to look in the general direction of downtown Boston and, somewhere in the heart of it, South Station. Seconds went by. The woman didn't make another move and didn't answer. Sadie could see her chest heaving and hear her breathing. She couldn't bear it.

"Listen, if you don't have the cash on you, I can help out."

"Oh, you're a good girl." The woman pulled a tissue out of her pocket and blew her nose. Her huge hand was trembling.

The poor thing was older than Sadie had imagined, she could see that now. Her shoulders more stooped, her eyes opaque, the skin loose on her face and arms. Her hair was dark, but that meant nothing. Just that she dyed it. All things considered, she must be Sadie's age. Oh, no, she must be older. It was the way she'd barreled down the street that threw a person off. Sadie had friends like that, decrepit on the outside but lungs like bellows and heart strong as a horse. Her own mother. At ninety, in a hospital bed, with cancer eating every part of her, her heart did not give up for days.

"It'll be okay," Sadie said. She wondered if Uncle and Auntie would expect her to put an arm around the woman now or pat her hand. In the hospital, she'd held her mother's hand for hours on end, afraid to let go. "Semicomatose," the nurse had said and shrugged. Twelve months later and Sadie still felt the imprint of her mother's palm against her own.

The woman balled up her tissue and tossed it into Mrs. Foster's garden. With an effort, Sadie held her tongue. "Naughty," the woman said and giggled. But Sadie didn't know which of them she meant.

"Want to see what I have here?" The woman reached down for her plastic bag. The night air was burrowing into Sadie's bones.

"Not now," she said.

"Don't worry. It's nothing bad."

With a small sigh, Sadie set her groceries down again, this time resting the sack against her leg. Then watched as the woman pulled out a pale piece of fabric.

"My nightie. Sweet, don't you think?" She held it up by the ribbon straps and draped it on her bosom like a bib. The style was what Sadie and her friends used to call a baby doll. Meant for some cute young thing, and this one looked to be three sizes, at the least, too small.

"I bought it at Sears. Full price, but I don't care." She smoothed the nightie over her chest. "When I sleep over, I like to make a good impression. My mother, rest her soul, taught me that. And, by the by"—she pointed a finger in Sadie's face—"you want to remember it, too.

"Don't worry about me."

The woman nodded. "I knew you'd see it my way. But I was telling you. The Haddads always put me up in a cozy room. Used to be the nursery. For a joke, I tell them I'm their baby. Anyways, if you know Retta, you know she does everything just so, embroidered pillowcases, mags on a little table by the bed, jellied mints in this dish she's got, shaped like a shell. Flowers, if you please, in a yellow vase on the dresser. Oh, that gal, she's a doll. *Don't you be a stranger*, she says to me. And Emile, he always plants a kiss before

I go to bed." She tapped her cheek. "I don't mind telling you, it's okay with me. A good-looking man like him. Of course, it's a while I haven't seen them."

"How long has it been?" Sadie asked, to hold up her end of the conversation.

"We're family, we don't keep track. All that matters is they treat me like a queen. Fresh orange juice and blueberry pancakes in the morning with real maple syrup. Not that I expect a fuss. You'll see"—she stuffed her nightgown back into her bag. "I'm used to waiting on myself."

"There's a phone booth on Jefferson," Sadie suggested. It was important to get things back on track.

"Oh, no, dear." She laughed as if Sadie had said something witty. "Half the time those don't work. Believe you me, I know. Thirty years I worked for the phone company. We'll call from your house." She hooked her arm in Sadie's and brought her lips close to Sadie's ear. "Anyways, darling, I'm dying to see where you finally settled down."

Sadie picked up her bundle and let herself be propelled down the street, her legs hurrying to keep up. Houses with lights on and shades up went by. The Kellehers' teenage girl on the phone; Old Man Palmquist in pajamas watching TV; in the white colonial with geranium pots outside, a shadow rocking behind kitchen curtains—probably that nice Mrs. Miller nursing her new baby. And here Sadie was, outside, in the dark, with this strange woman and, if she couldn't come up with a good excuse, about to let her in the house.

"Am I going too fast for you, honey?" the woman asked.

Sadie didn't want to be a baby. "I'm all right."

"I know you are, don't I know that?" the woman said, but she slowed the pace and squeezed in closer.

"I want to tell you something, dear." Sadie could feel the woman's warm breath on her neck and smell her toilet water. Midnight in Paris, she would have said, except it was years since she'd seen it in a drugstore. Four dollars for three ounces in a dark blue bottle. She used to save up and buy it every Christmas for her mother. "Oh," her mother would say in her broken English, "too much I gonna smell good!" One thing about her mother, she'd been a lady, stayed in at night, tended to her family, didn't dress showy. Not 'til she got old and started wearing fancy barrettes in her wispy hair and prints in every color of the rainbow. Those were the years she took to whining and finding fault.

"Are you listening, dear?" The woman pinched Sadie's arm. "You shouldn't run around alone at night. Folks might get the wrong idea."

"An old lady like me?" Sadie laughed, she couldn't help it.

"You're not so old, I take it back I ever said that. Just remember, if gossip gets a foothold, the boys won't ask you out. Unless they're after you know what." She made a little clucking sound and reached up to smooth back Sadie's thinning hair. "Who's gonna tell you these things if I don't?"

They were face to face now, come to a stop. The woman's eyes were familiar as Sadie's own eyes in the mirror, or as her little sister's who had died. *The night plays tricks,* Sadie thought.

And then she saw a man ahead hurrying their way. The woman saw, too. "Pay no attention," she said to Sadie. "People make up the most awful stories."

The man lifted his arm as if hailing a cab. "Auntie Lillian!" Sadie could make out his ponytail and horn-rimmed glasses.

The woman, who had stepped away from Sadie, was crowding her again, burying her face on Sadie's shoulder, clutching her 'round the waist. "How does that person know my name?"

Sadie took another look. "It's your cousin," she said. The woman held on tighter, the weight of her on Sadie's shoulder and back. Sadie nudged her. "Your cousin," she repeated. "Say hello."

Emile stood in front of them, his hands in the back pockets of his jeans. "This is silly, Aunt Lillian. You're coming back with me."

"I'm not!" She was balanced on her own two feet now, her jaw thrust out. Sadie had started to say something, but the woman drowned her out.

Emile peered in her direction. "Aunt Sadie?"

She smiled. "Hello, Emile." *Rescued,* she thought, ready to scurry home. "Take care, Lillian," she said as pleasantly as she knew how. "I'm glad you found your family."

Lillian scowled. "You never even told me your name. I had to hear it from my cousin here." Her hand twitched in his direction.

And what about you? Sadie was about to say but caught herself. She wouldn't get roped in again. As for Emile, he must know enough not to take seriously anything this woman said. But, bless him, he'd shown up in the nick of time. When she baked her Christmas sweets this year, she'd send a tray over to the Haddads.

With a grimace, Emile nodded good-night, slid Lillian's heavy purse off her arm and took her by the elbow. "Retta's waiting."

As Sadie hung back, Lillian let herself be led away. But after a few steps, she looked back. "Sadie," she said, "don't make me go."

A sharp pain in her chest caught Sadie off guard. *Don't make me go.* What her mother had said when Sadie moved her out of their house and into the nursing home. "I had to," Sadie explained to herself and to anyone who'd listen. In those last weeks when her mother was still with her, all night Sadie had been afraid to sleep. In case her mother got out of bed and fell. And even with Sadie's help, she might not make it to the bathroom in time. Sadie remembered the diapers she'd resorted to and the accidents on the rug. "I'll visit you every day," she'd promised. And she had. And later in the hospital. "God punish you," her mother had said. Her body was weak but her will was still strong, and she was calling down curses on her daughter's head.

Emile had halted, too, but still had a grip on Lillian's arm. "Let me explain."

"You don't have to, Emile. I'll just be on my way."

"We made an appointment for her, tomorrow with a specialist. She doesn't want to go, she's scared of doctors. But it's not up to her, is it?" He cocked his head—"You see how things are."

Lillian was paying close attention as if Emile were offering up a tasty slice of gossip.

Sadie was tired. If only she could sit down. She looked into the distance, trying to catch a glimpse of her front porch. She'd left the light on. If she could see it, she could believe she'd make it home. The porch, an old-fashioned wraparound, was where her mother sat on summer days and on hot evenings, and visitors sat when they came by. Most usually it had been Uncle in one rocker and Auntie in another, and later Auntie by herself. If Sadie narrowed her eyes, she could almost see the three of them looking around, asking each other what was keeping her.

Emile had stepped out from under the street lamp. It was hard to see his face. "We got her here this afternoon," he said. "After supper, Retta polished her nails for her, and made sure she'd gone to bed, but when we checked on her, she was gone." Shadows moved behind him. Sadie didn't like the thought that someone might be listening, but she was almost sure they were alone.

"Auntie Lillian"—Emile's voice rang out in the dark—"it was naughty, scaring us like that."

"I don't care. I'm going to Sadie's house. We're best friends now." With sudden energy, she threw off his arm and lurched toward Sadie. "Emile's a good boy," she said, "but he's not very smart." She dropped her heavy head on Sadie's shoulder. "Us gals have gotta stick like glue."

If only, Sadie thought, she'd put off her little bit of shopping 'til tomorrow. "You should listen to Emile," she said and tried to squirm away. Much good he was, fidgeting with his glasses. "She likes you," he said to her at last. Then to Lillian. "Do you want to go home with Sadie? Would that be fun? I'll pick you up first thing in the morning." His eyes shifted back to Sadie. "I guess you and us, we're almost family anyhow."

Lillian rocked back and forth in a little dance step. "Sadie, we can stay up late and gab about the boys, we can drink hot chocolate with marshmallows. You'll see how pretty I look in my new nightie."

Sadie shook her head.

"Okay, you wear the nightie, but don't get it dirty. I can't be washing up after you all the time. If you're a good girl, I'll tuck you into bed.

"Emile." Sadie spoke sternly. He was staring at the sidewalk.

Lillian pulled at her sleeve. "I'm waiting," she said. "But I haven't got all night."

Sadie wanted to run, but she forced herself to put a hand on Emile's arm. "I can't do this," she said.

"Are you sure?"

Sadie thought about the ice cream she'd promised herself before going to bed. "I'm sure."

Lillian turned to Emile and rolled her eyes. "Missie here is always out for herself."

Emile laid his hand on Lillian's back. "We're going home. Retta will make you hot chocolate, she knows how you like it." He took her by the arm, and they started walking.

"Good night, Lillian," Sadie called out. She didn't answer.

Sadie watched until distance reduced the two figures to dark silhouettes, then just to pencil strokes. And then not even that. They must have turned off Pheasant, she thought, but waited another minute to be sure. When the coast seemed clear, she reached down for her grocery bag, cradled it against her chest, and headed home. It was late to be out on the street, only a few houses now with lights on. Good thing, she had companions, Uncle on one side of her, Auntie on the other. She was glad now she hadn't bought a whole quart of jam. As she told them, it would have been more than she could carry. They murmured something. They seemed to understand.

House Calls

The night after the funeral Father Michael was in bed, his wife under him, his ass going to town. He was just hitting his stride when some little thing—a hiss or could be a tremor—caught him off guard. He listed left in time to see one wall of the bedroom dissolve and Aggie, herself, stumble in. Father shuddered and reared. His wife, eyes shut tight, urged him on.

Aggie, meanwhile, had lost her footing. Suspended several inches above the carpet, she was treading air, grabbing for the top of the highboy, trying to backpedal. "Forgive me, Father," she croaked, her words half swallowed in an eddy of wind that stirred Father's beard and whirled her back through the wall. Quick as a gasp, another apology threaded its way under the door—"Edna, so sorry."

But Edna hadn't seen her or heard her; had overlooked her even when Aggie was alive; knew only that her husband, again, was quitting early.

Once Aggie had had a chance at romance, when she was young and pretty for a little while, her brown hair falling softly to her shoulders. The young man offered marriage, but her uncles said no. What could she do? Father dead, mother deferring always to her brothers-in-law.

Aggie's sisters hadn't been surprised—"He's not even Lebanese," they pointed out. But that wasn't it. Aggie overheard her uncles in the kitchen, clearing their throats, saying "think of it this way." Would they sell a bolt of damaged yard goods in their shop? God forbid. They were men of honor. Then could they foist their niece off on a blameless stranger? The day would come, he'd curse them and raise his hand against her. Aggie held her breath until her favorite uncle had the final say. "I wouldn't want my son yoked to a cripple."

It happened when she was eight years old and ill with a fever. A doctor came to the house, bearing a black bag out of which he drew a syringe and let lightening into her veins. Her right arm shot up at the elbow, never to straighten again; her right hand twisted into a grimace that held.

Aggie toughed it out. Through grade school and high school and after, her affliction preceded her like a town crier publishing pain. She might have keeled over. Instead, her will clenched like muscle. She'd prove she could do as much as any woman. Could handle a dustpan and broom, wash dishes, change beds; could flip pancakes, peel celery, even roll grape leaves; could tote laundry down to the cellar and cartons of Christmas ornaments up to the attic; could open and shut the stiff legs of the card table, drive a standard shift, tie a bow, iron a man's shirt, perfectly.

What a helpmate she might have been, she knew that for a fact. She could have changed a baby, nursed it at her breast, cradled it in her arm and never let it fall.

Of course, there were limits—she accepted them as humblings

from God. She could not zip up the back of her dress or hook her own bra; at table she could not cut her own meat. When her favorite nephew blew out the candles on his birthday cake, she could clap with only one hand, which was nearly no clapping at all.

Hard physical truth made Aggie a realist for keeps. On the last afternoon of her life, her body closing shop, her heart running on empty, she still knew fact from fiction. "She's a little better," one niece whispered, stooping to study the sallow face against the pillow.

"No, dear, I'm dying."

Irritating to the end, that young lady's wishful thinking.

Father Michael was as level-headed as the next guy. He had no truck with visitors from the grave. He knew a nightmare when he had one. The thing was not to let it prey. But the day after Aggie's call, he tugged at one eyebrow, tugged at the other, and blamed her that next Sunday's homily wasn't going well. As moments passed and nothing to show for them, he played with his pencil, spinning it across his desk, rolling it off the edge and catching it, drumming it against his teeth, eraser to enamel. Musicians had it good, he thought. If God in his mercy hadn't called him, he could have played the sax, led a band, even been a vocalist. In seminary, the most reverends couldn't say enough about his voice. Eyes closed, he threw back his head and lifted his pencil like a baton. "Sleepy-time gal," he hummed, "you're turning night into day . . ."

"That's nice, Father."

His body jerked, his eyes opened a crack. The news was bad: wrinkled cheeks, silly smile, arm fancy as a serpent. With three damp fingers bunched in homage to the Trinity, Father Michael crossed himself. From right to left, of course—he was no papist.

Quickly, Aggie followed his lead, propelling her right hand with her left, up, down, east, west. "She mocks me," thought Father Michael. "And her so timid." It must be a jinni had got hold of her body. *Just say begone,* he prompted himself. *Say in the name of Christ and all the seraphim.* He took a breath.

"Oh, Father!" Aggie hurried to forestall him. "There's nothing so sacred as the marriage bed, don't I know that? But it's like this. One minute I'm saying to myself, what I wouldn't give for a heart-to-heart with Father, but probably he's turned in already, and next thing I know, I'm smack-dab in your bedroom."

With all his strength, Father Michael willed her away.

"You see how it was, Father?"

What had he ever done to her? What was she after?

Aggie leaned closer, fluttering papers on his desk.

This must be some kind of test. If he sat still until it was over and didn't cry out, God would reward him. "I'm a good man," he thought.

Aggie circled the desk until she was only inches away from him. He held his breath and tried not to stare. Her deformity. He might have known it carried a curse.

"I worry about you, Father. You're working too hard, you're so pale."

He still didn't answer.

Despite herself, Aggie was getting annoyed.

"Father, cat got your tongue?"

He smiled a frightened smile. Then jumped in terror as a knock sounded at the door. With a shrug of disappointment, Aggie giant-stepped through the window and launched herself over the shrubbery. Another stride landed her in the crotch of an apple tree, where she paused to scratch her leg and think things over. Bottom line, she was getting nowhere. But it was hard to find Father alone, and meanwhile time was bleeding away and her with so many good deeds on her agenda.

Her sisters had called her Saint Aggie. That wasn't fair, though she did often think how good she'd been to people, better than they deserved. Take the way she'd catered to her uncles' widows, even the one who acted high and mighty. "Yes, Auntie, I'll take you food shopping," Aggie used to say to whichever of the two was on the phone. "Sure, I'll pass by the post office." She brought them native corn in August and brown eggs from the farm, and, when they were on sale, the bloomers the old ladies liked and the stockings that attached to garters.

But with the years Aggie had grown prickly. By the time father, mother, uncles, and aunts were dead and she was left the oldest of her generation, she'd recast herself as matriarch. With that office came the duty to keep her family on the straight and narrow. "Over my dead body," she said when a sister thought of bleaching her hair, a niece took a shine to an Irishman, a sister-in-law talked up frozen dinners. The older she got, the less need she felt to curb her tongue.

"How's my cake?" her cousin asked after helping her to a slice. "Dry as dust," she replied, washing the crumbs down with loud gulps of tea. When her nephew's wife walked out on him, Aggie announced, "I wouldn't shit on the best part of her." At her brother-in-law's wake, she prayed God, just under her breath, to "bury the asshole deeper."

"And you're the one who goes to church?" Her sisters were beside themselves. They only wished her precious priest could hear her now.

Three years earlier, when Father Michael had taken over at Saint Nicholas, he'd found Aggie already bucking for the role of number-one lady parishioner. Under his inspiration, she made it her own, beating down all competition. After she was laid to rest, Father Michael counted over her virtues: how gladly she sold raffles table-to-table at church suppers or minded the church office when the secretary was on vacation. How cheerfully she dropped by the Byblos Bakery for holy bread or made a run to Cedars Nursery for extra pots of Easter lilies. If a parishioner succumbed to cancer or old age, Father could rely on Aggie's arriving early to help the women's circle prepare the mercy meal. "Ladies," she'd chirp, pulling a flowered apron out of a paper sack, "I'm at your beck and call."

And always it was "Yes, Father" or "You're right, Father." Not like others he could mention. But she'd seen right through that crowd. "You're too good for them, Father."

Aggie swung down from the apple tree. She'd laid her plans. See to poor Eddie, that was important. But first she'd look in on her sister.

Kate was sitting on a footstool in Aggie's bedroom. Behind her an ancient radiator, painted gray to match the walls; beside her, Aggie's iron bed that used to be their mother's. Through the window, the March sun laid a pale hand on piles of papers and cartons of belongings Kate had tugged down from Aggie's closet shelf or hauled down from Aggie's corner of the attic. Like someone with a bonfire in mind.

Dust tickled Kate's throat as she peered into limp manila envelopes, unfolded crumbling obituaries, dumped stray keys and hoards of buttons on the rug (*like I've nothing better to do with my time,* she thought.) As time passed, she picked up speed, tossing out almost everything—yellowed wedding invitations, some for people on their third marriage now (*and me still on the vine*); a 1972 calendar with holy days printed in red, birthdays circled in ballpoint (*Aggie, for you, mailing out cards, reminding people of what they'd as soon forget*); her mother's recipes for raw kibbi (*lucky we didn't all die a horrible retching death*) and lamb with okra (*slimy stuff*). From now on, Kate planned to live (*like any normal person*) on hamburgers and American chop suey.

Then, at the bottom of a hatbox, something different. Kate lifted out a packet of letters mottled with age and bound with faded ribbon. "Billy Dews," she cooed, sure they weren't. But foreign stamps? Arabic script? How could anyone know what they said, and why, please, would anyone hang on to them? A two-handed jump shot landed the bunch in the trash bag.

"What the dickens are you up to?"

With a little burp, Kate toppled against the ribs of the radiator before hitting the floor. When she looked up, Aggie was sitting with knees squeezed together on the edge of the bed, one shoulder hunched, one hand perpetually clutched. The two-piece print they'd buried her in was riding up over her knees as if she'd put on weight. Her mouth was going.

"Look at you." Aggie scowled, her neck thrust forward like a rooster's, in that ugly way Kate could never abide. *Some day,* she used to tell herself, some day she'd put two fingers against Aggie's chin and push back her face. Playing for time, Kate gripped the radiator and hoisted herself to her feet. Her elbow hurt, and so did her behind.

With her good hand, Aggie pointed. "You got history there, letters from before I was born. Don't you dare throw them out."

Aggie's know-it-all tone, unsubdued by the grave, set Kate's nerves on edge. Sixty years old, and all her life she'd had to answer to this one and that one. After her mother died, she should have moved out. No matter what anyone said, she could have managed. She righted the stool with a thump and went back about her business. There was nothing to say.

Aggie got the picture. "No use." She tugged at her skirt, then pushed off and bicycled once in the air before touching down on the far side of the trash bag.

Not bad, thought Kate, for someone who'd gone through all of junior high and high school excused from gym class. But next thing she knew, Aggie was reaching toward the sack with her good hand.

Kate got there first. "Oh, no you don't."

That afternoon, Aggie found Eddie in the kitchen of his flat, pressing his good trousers. She stood to one side watching him struggle with the seams. Dear heart, he didn't know the first thing about it, and why should he?

"What the hell?" Out of the corner of his eye, Eddie had noticed a shape half hidden by the fridge.

"It's only me, dear." Aggie crept out to show herself. Poor boy, his hands were trembling. He set the iron down, almost knocking it to the floor. "Only me," she crooned, soothing him as if he were her baby.

"Right." His voice was pitched high, tinged with hysteria. He put his hand to his mouth and coughed. "Right you are." Aggie thought she could hear the first jolt of astonishment giving way.

He'd been through this before. His mother had come to him at midnight. The night of the day she'd died. He'd been sitting in front of the fireplace, and a white dove had appeared on the hearth. She'd stayed with him 'til dawn. He hadn't told anyone.

Aggie moved a step closer. "I can't rest for worrying about you, dear. How you've no one to cook hot meals, share your burdens, sew your buttons." It takes a woman, she thought, eying the trail of spots at her feet where something orange and sticky had dripped on the linoleum. She hoped he was listening.

"Poor Aunt Aggie," he thought. Even in death, her arm hadn't relaxed.

"I mean what I say, dear. You need a wife. A good girl this time. But she won't drop in your lap." He was like his mother, Aggie thought. Counting on miracles. "You've got to step out"—she swung her hips—"mix with people, get in the swim."

Next to his mother, Aunt Aggie had loved him the best. But she had a way of getting things wrong. "I'm not ready for another wife."

At last, Aggie thought, he was paying attention.

"I'm not saying be in a rush, dear. No, be smart, look the field over before you settle on anyone."

He came out from behind the ironing board, and began pacing the few feet to the stove and back. "They won't come running. I'm not such a hot catch."

Aggie followed him with her eyes. "Make sure she's a good homemaker, dear. But someone with a job—let her bring in a few dollars this time."

Eddie crossed to the table cluttered, as Aggie had noticed, with old newspapers, a sweatshirt, and running shoes. He pulled out a chair. For the first time, he looked her full in the face. "Auntie, sit and listen a minute."

"And do like the big shots do, dear. Have a prenuptial agreement."

"But that's for people with money."

She smiled. "Never mind, dear. God is good. And it's not just the smart that get rich. Who knows? He may send good fortune your way and, if he does,"—she smoothed her dress under her and sat down at the table—"we don't want some whore picking your pocket."

"Aunt Aggie, you might as well know." He planted his palms on the table. "I still love Wanda. All I keep thinking is how to make her come back."

Something hot tore through Aggie's chest. Her cheeks felt stiff, her tongue heavy in her mouth. "Eddie, dear, I know you better than you know yourself. Please"—with her good hand she brought the other to her heart—"you can't love that thing."

He crossed his arms and turned toward the window. "That's no way to talk." She remembered him as a child, digging in about something or other, folding his arms in that same little-boy way. But he wasn't a boy any more. Aggie noticed his hair was thinning, his skin loose at the nape of his neck. "You're like my own son I never had," she said. His shoulders slumped.

"I know."

"But from day one,"—she tapped the table—"you let that woman walk all over you." Aggie settled back in her chair. "You've no backbone, dear. I only tell you this because I love you."

Eddie spun around. "Why can't you stop spoiling things?"

When all she wanted was to help. But Aggie forgave him. "Eddie, dear,"—she had a new thought—"do you want me to speak to her, to put in a word for you?"

He eyed her. "Why would you do that, Aunt Aggie?"

"All I want is my boy to be happy."

That sounded all right. He didn't think God would let her come back just to lie to him. "I'm going to trust you," he said. "But listen"—he was all business now—"don't you scare her. Talk to her nice. Tell her if she comes back, I'll try to do better." Aggie groaned but Eddie would not be put off. "And here's the big thing. You've got to say you're sorry. You had no right that time—what you said about her makeup and her movie magazines." His tone softened. "Don't you see, Aunt Aggie? You here—it's like a miracle, like God wants me to have another chance. Tell her you were wrong to make trouble. Let her hear it out of your mouth."

"So that's what you want of your auntie?" Her voice was barely audible. "The one who loves you better than her own life."

Eddie's concerns were now firmly in the forefront of Aggie's mind. She saw that things had come to a dangerous pass. She'd talk to that Wanda, yes she'd do that. And she wouldn't worry about scaring her either. Let her tremble in her boots! Let her drop dead in a faint! Let her fat face turn purple, and her eyes bulge like eggs. Father Michael and Kate would have to wait their turn.

Wanda's living room, nobody there. Aggie was half relieved. But no, she wouldn't shirk. Making free of the apartment, she floated silently through the kitchen *(filthy!)*, the bedroom *((that anyone could live like that!)* and into the steamy bathroom. Wanda was lounging in the tub, most of her hidden under drifts of bubble bath, like a strawberry cake topped with marshmallow icing. Her breasts, pink from the heat, were bobbing under her chin, her eyes were closed, her frosted hair was bobby-pinned on top of her head. Beside the tub sat a matching aquamarine hopper, exactly placed for intimate chat. Quietly Aggie claimed it. As if on cue, one slim hand with scarlet-lacquered nails emerged through the bubble bath, one tapered finger began picking at a spot on the chin. Wanda opened her eyes, and almost stopped breathing.

"You."

"In person."

Wanda's eyes darted around the bathroom—fogged up mirror, limp towels, pantyhose pooled on the floor. No help anywhere. "Hail Mary," she whispered, her gaze riveted on a jar of cotton balls.

"Listen, you, I've a message from Eddie."

Wanda pressed her palms against her ears. "La, la, la," she sang out. The bubbles around her were collapsing now. "Pft," they said, "pft."

"I'm here to tell you, the boy wants you home."

"You want *me* to go back to Eddie?"

"As long as you mend your trashy ways."

Wanda beat the water with her fists until it sloshed onto the floor.

Outside, it was already dark, and the air was damp. Straddling the peak of the roof, her back against the cold brick of the chimney, Aggie shivered and thought of Eddie. Some day he'd thank her. Then curiosity got the better of her. She craned her neck over the eave and down a story. Through a second-floor window, she spotted Wanda sprawled on her bed, clutching a towel to her chest and dialing. "Please, God," Aggie prayed, "don't let it be Eddie or, if it is, don't let him be home."

Kate chalked it up to the usual routine: every few weeks Wanda on the phone, keeping a pipeline open. In case Eddie hooked up with someone, she wanted to know. Of course, Aggie would slam down the receiver, but Kate was always civil.

"What's up?" she asked.

"Oh, Aunt Kate!" Her words came in a rush. "I'm soaking in the tub, trying to calm my nerves, which I don't have to tell you how they are these days, and just for a minute I doze off, but, my bad luck, I dream about Aunt Aggie!" She paused. "Are you still there?"

"Go ahead."

"It was awful! She pops out of a cloud, and she's all pasty white."

Kate was relieved. Maybe it hadn't been hallucination, after all, or what she dreaded most, the beginnings of senility. Maybe Aggie really was on the prowl. "I wouldn't put it past her," she thought.

"But here's the thing of it, Aunt Kate. She said Eddie's pining for me to go back to him. He can't eat, he can't sleep. What do you think?"

"Beats me."

"You know, that dream could be a message."

"Who from?"

"The Blessed Virgin."

"Herself?"

"Well, things like that happen."

. . .

Before noon the next day, the phone rang again.

"It's Father Michael, Kate."

"What can I do for you, Father?" She was checking the contents of her purse, getting ready to hurry out the door.

"Kate, you put up a brave front but, believe me, I miss her, too." Kate propped the phone against her ear, found an emery board in her purse, and started filing down a nail that had caught on her hose when she pulled them on after her shower. "So full of good works," Father Michael was saying, "our Aggie of blessed memory." He waited but she didn't answer. "Kate, the Lord is counting on us to lay down our sorrow and take up his cross. To be good and faithful workers in his vineyard. He's counting on you, Kate, to put your hand to the plow."

Kate examined her other nails. His voice made her tired. "Meaning what, Father?"

"The church, Kate."

Kate sat down on the arm of an easy chair and crossed her legs at the ankle. "Father, I'm not my sister." And at that very moment, Kate had an inspiration. Perhaps from the blessed Virgin.

"Father, you read Arabic, don't you?"

"Of course."

"Then you'll appreciate what Aggie's left you."

An illuminated manuscript leapt to mind. He knew she wouldn't stint. "Your sister was a saint, Kate. I hope you realize."

Kate stood up and looked around for her car keys.

"You bet."

More and more, Aggie got lost in dreams, forgot the things that needed doing. That wasn't like her. Everything an effort. If only she could close her eyes and hush her thoughts. Then she would heal. The problem was she couldn't trust Kate to see to things: keep a proper house, keep up the family name.

"What did you do with the afghan on my bed?" That's how she greeted Kate the next time.

"That old thing?" Kate said, a lot calmer than she'd been before. It was the first visit knocked you off your pins. She went back to her novel. "It's in the dump by now."

"Handmade!" wailed Aggie. "Mama crocheted it for me when I was a little girl."

Kate looked up. "Then you got your money's worth."

Silence.

"And where's the braided rug should be by my bed?"

Kate tossed her book aside and reached for a mint patty. "Gone. I threw it out."

"You threw it out? But it had wool from Mama's coat and Baba's suit."

"There's your problem." Kate nibbled at the candy. "Always living in the past."

The next time Aggie dropped in, Kate was stretched on the recliner in the sun parlor. Aggie thought how little time she'd ever had for lounging. "What about the piccalilli I put up last summer?" she said. "And my pickled turnips? Going to waste, I don't doubt it. You know, there's plenty people be thrilled to have what you got in stock."

Kate checked her watch and clicked on the TV. "Time for *Jeopardy.*"

Another time, Aggie planted herself behind Kate who was warming milk at the stove. The flame too high.

"It's gonna burn," Aggie warned.

"Good!" said Kate. "That's how I damn well like it."

"That's how she likes it." Aggie listened to the plop, plop of the kitchen faucet. What's so hard about calling a plumber, she wanted to say.

For once, she kept her mouth shut. Withdrew, like a sea creature into its shell. She'd tried so hard, and yet nothing she said seemed to make an impression. You might as well talk to your underwear. But it was hard to let go, to give up her dream of making her family right and things right for her family.

Not much time left now, she sensed. Aggie wandered through their house, Kate's house, brushing up against the living room furniture, watching the sunlight scribble on the wallpaper, listening to the antique clock tick for attention. She hadn't meant to waste minutes bickering with Kate. She'd meant something else. Meant to say life was hard, who knew that better than she did? But there were rules that made it easier, that drew a thick line between right and wrong, friend and enemy, family and outsider. All that hard-won wisdom, shot through with ancient promises and threats. It couldn't die with her.

But when she saw Kate in the kitchen again, everything she'd meant to say fell away.

"Kate, the faucet's still leaking, it's a wonder you can stand it!" This time Kate heard Aggie like someone speaking underwater, the words muffled, impossible to make out.

For days, Aggie had been dodging Eddie. True, she couldn't totally ignore him, not with him on the lookout. Always now, his head tilted upwards like someone watching for a flash of wings.

"Don't worry," she'd whisper and be gone.

"Wait," he'd call out. And then it got so he was afraid to summon her back, afraid of the answers he'd hear.

Strange how passing over had not freed her. Not from Eddie, not from Kate, and not at all from Father Michael. "I wouldn't bother the dear man except it's on business," she told herself. She couldn't admit it was mostly make-business. "But know what it looks like?" she asked herself one day. "Like Father don't care for my company now." When she tried to get his attention, he was like a sleeper slapping at a mosquito, or a child in the schoolyard blinking away a cinder. Girl and woman, she had faced up to everything, but these days Father was always looking offstage, somewhere behind her or over her head.

The day came she caught him off guard. He'd been dozing in an easy chair by the window of his study and was just coming awake. Aggie stood over him and hurried to have her say.

"Father, listen please." He half opened his eyes. "In my will, Father, a little something for the church. You know that already, don't you?" He grinned an empty grin, nothing but space behind it. A person could reach into his mouth, Aggie imagined, and waggle a handful of fingers. Could crawl through and come out the other side.

"Now Father"—she pulled herself back to the matter at hand—"don't go thinking I don't trust my folks. Kate's got her faults, but she's no crook." Father's smile was collapsing like a sand tunnel giving way. Aggie took a deep breath. "I just believe in person-to-person, Father, you and me. So's I can explain things myself." Father Michael, his face closed, gave no indication that he understood. Aggie hurtled ahead.

"Here's the story, Father. I've left ten thousand to the seminary. Young priests, we need them. You said so yourself. To keep the church alive, bring the children in, maybe teach them Arabic. I don't like to see so much of the liturgy turned into English, Father. I should think you could speak to the bishop. I know, for a fact, the archmandrite sees it my way." Father Michael leaned forward and put his palms on his knees, as if about to rise. "Wait, Father!" He sat back, let out a sigh, and Aggie saw a plume of dust billow around him. "You get my meaning, do you Father?" The dust settled on his skin, his clothes. "Father?" He stared at his shoelaces. "How times change," Aggie mused. "Used to be Father talked and talked and I was the one listened."

"There's more, Father. Some dollars coming in on a little investment. For remembering my loved ones in Sunday prayers. By name, Father. Each one, the month they died, it's all spelled out. My mother, my father, my Uncle Abe, my Uncle Yusef, their wives—Sophie and Madeline. Did you ever meet Madeline, Father? No, she was before your time. Well, you were lucky. My sister Katreen, my sister Helen,—younger than me, Father, but I outlived them both. And of course, my brother Chick, God rest his soul. He died in springtime, April. Another six weeks, he was retiring from the navy yard. Think of it, Father, six little weeks. But things never did go smooth for Chick."

Her eyes were wet, but Father Michael didn't notice. On Aggie's earlier visits, he'd been speechless out of fear. Terrified that she had come to drag him down with her, for company, into the grave. Or, since she could maybe read his heart, to quiz him on its secrets. None of that had happened, so now it was simple annoyance clogging his throat. What was she always going on about? Father's thoughts strayed to the church picnic coming up before you knew it, the troublemakers on the parish council, his blood pressure (the doctor had warned him), Edna's shopping sprees, the bishop's visit in September. And every time he went off, Aggie became dim and her voice faded in and out like a radio before it gives up the ghost. After a while, he could hardly make out a word and she'd flattened to shadow.

"Father Michael!" Aggie called, but he heard only a hum. Already he'd slipped away to his desk and was putting in a call to someone named Ida, asking her to round up donations for the upcoming raffle.

"Oh, not her." Aggie thought. "Not that toad face with the blue hair." "Father!" She raised her voice. "Can't you hear me?" He never looked up.

And yet she couldn't walk away. He was off the phone now. Aggie watched him sort and stack papers on his desk, pausing over a bulky envelope. When it had first arrived, he'd glanced at its contents just long enough to be disappointed, then thrown it aside. Now, seeing it where it waited on his desk, he was mildly curious, opened the flap, and shook out a bunch of letters. Aggie knew them at once. Her heart beat with happiness. Father Michael disengaged one letter from its envelope, ran his eye down the page, then pulled out another and another. Translating quickly, he took in a few sentences here, a paragraph there.

September 1899:
I write at the behest of your honorable father. Happy news! Your Uncle Rashid's daughter Miriam has married a village boy of good family, your old playmate, Boulus

Mitri. Tomorrow they sail for America in the company of his brother and three kinsmen. May they prosper and, God willing, return in safety to their parents. And may you lead the way home, my young hero, covered in glory.

March 1900:

The tax collectors plague us, my son. Like locusts they eat their full and ask for more. These are your father's words. He says, Oh my son, the light of your mother's eye, when you return—if God pleases—to gladden our hearts, you will help me dig a new well.

November 1903:

Umm Michel, the schoolmaster's wife, she who loved you and praised your diligence, has suffered a grave loss. Her husband, may God receive his soul, has surrendered his days on this earth.

July 1905:

Rashid Yazbeck has returned from America and built for his parents a fine stone house with a roof of red tile. How fortunate they are, how they laugh and hug themselves!

June 1906:

Blessings on the birth of your firstborn. Your honored father says, do not grieve that she is a girl child. Your father says, may her groom have a face like the sun and own many hecates . . . May your wife live to bear you a dozen sons.

December 1908:

All the young men are now fled from the village. They are wise. Why should they risk their lives to defend the Sultan? But in each house, the women weep and call out.

July 1910:

Your father asks, another daughter, my son? It is perhaps the water in America. Here the springs are pure, and the air one breathes gives health. Your mother prays God to send you once before she dies. We will feast. . . .

Father Michael had read enough. He called his wife, thrust the letters into her hands.

"Oh, Father, save them to remember me by," cried Aggie.

"What's this stuff?" Edna demanded.

Father Michael was reaching again for the phone. "You can dump it," he said.

Trouser bottoms and oxfords showing under his vestments, Father Michael looked down on his congregation. Most of the regulars were there despite the ice storm that, overnight, had blackened fruit blossoms and blasted the shoots of spring bulbs. A few guests had filed in, too. Kate, for instance, in the first pew to his left. He might never see her in church again, he thought, but not even Kate could say no to a forty-day memorial for her sister. Beside Kate, he recognized her nephew Eddie. The rest of the family, nieces and their children, another nephew, all lived out of state and probably weren't coming. The slick roads, that would be their alibi. On

Eddie's other side, in a fuzzy pink jacket, was a blond woman Father couldn't place at first.

Aggie was there too, seated on the step leading to the apron of the altar. Practically at Father Michael's feet though he didn't notice her. Kate—her mind half on new curtains, half on memories of Aggie walking her to kindergarten, squeezing her hand 'til it hurt—didn't see her either. Neither did Eddie, though Aggie saw him well enough, Wanda beside him, almost in his lap. Across the aisle sat Edna, looking angry. Maybe she had reason.

Aggie glanced from face to face, hoping to catch someone's eye. When that failed, she leaned heavily on her good hand, shimmied up a step, then rolled over on her knees. The effort made Aggie's head swim, and her heart race, and still she was stalled, her hind side to the congregation, her face toward the altar and the iconostasis in front of it. "Mother of God," she cried. An icon of the Virgin Mary, no doubt with worries of her own, did not look down. In the adjacent panel, a dashing Saint George, his steed pawing the air, was forever impaling a fire-breathing dragon, forever awaiting applause. Nearby, the four Evangelists, not impressed by such derring-do, maintained a dignified silence.

"Mark my words," Aggie cried. With effort, she rotated her body, then rocked back on her heels, straightening her spine, searching for family. She wanted to leave them something. The sanctuary was growing dark, blackness extinguishing each pale face.

"I must be dying," she thought.

"Forgive her all her transgressions, both voluntary and involuntary," prayed Father Michael. "May her memory be eternal," he intoned.

"May her memory be eternal," the cantor seconded.

"Amen," mouthed Kate, paying no attention. Eddie smiled, squeezed Wanda's hand.

"Through the intercession of our Most Holy and Virgin Lady, receive her into a place of verdure, a place of light."

Aggie closed her eyes.

When she opened them again, she was home, in the slip of garden behind the house. The sky was crayon blue, the air brimmed with sunlight. Close to earth, orange poppies with purple feelers glowed by the fence; tulips, startled into red and lemon yellow, shot up around her; pot-o'-gold sunned itself at her feet. Not the work of *her* hand. She'd always planted veggies, sprayed their leaves with bug killer, rooted out weeds, propped up stalks sprawled on the ground. Dear Chick, she'd never forget, had helped her stake them. Yet every year it was either brown spots on the lettuce, or squash with borers worming through their veins, or shriveled cucumbers wrung into grotesque shapes. So much wasted effort.

"I should have gone for color," Aggie thought, before the scent of lilac took her breath away.

I Got My Eye on You

Hour ago, Sissie caught the school bus with the others, but now she's back, sneaking along the side of her house, scrunched down low so her mama won't see her from the kitchen window. Miss Sissie doesn't dream I got my eye on her. Now she's running. Now she's behind the tool shed. She'll crouch there hugging herself to keep warm and lighting up a ciggie. Waiting for the house to empty out.

From my barrel chair, I can look out the window without her or anybody seeing. I don't want people staring in at me. Especially now I'm an old lady on my own. Who knows who could be hiding round the corner of the house or in the shrubbery. Killers, rapists, whackos who might take me for their mothers that they hated. I think about that sometimes, what would I do if one got in the house. "Listen," I'd say, "before you make a move, look close, I'm not your mama." The trick is act friendly, say "How about a cup of coffee while we talk this thing over?" Then make a run for it out the back. Of course, a real lunatic would cut me down in a minute with my own carving knife that I keep sharp or strangle me with

128

two feet of rope he brought along on purpose in his jacket pocket. So now you know why I put in dead bolts on the front door and the back, and locks on all the first-floor windows. When the sun goes down, I make the rounds, double check the latches, let down the blinds.

There's Sissie's mother, in high heels, getting in her car. She'll be off to her job at City Hall. Administrative something-something, she calls herself, but I'm betting it's just plain typing, answering the phone, and filing. Her husband and her brother, the two of them, they leave early for their garage they own. Yup, she's pulling out. Now Sissie'll go inside and watch TV all day and stuff her mouth with chips and other junk to give her blackheads.

Not just crazies. I can't abide the thought of anyone looking in my window and knowing when I'm eating or on the phone. One good thing, there's a huge rhodie out in front that hides me when I sit on the piazza in the summer. Through the leaves, I see the regulars. Poor Jack Conroy, who had the polio, half limping, half running, late for work as usual—he grabs the bus down at the corner; Elma Wieher, who went to school with me and stole my boyfriend in tenth grade—she's using a cane now for her arthritis but still takes her morning constitutional and still wears too much lipstick; in the afternoon, the O'Connell boy on his way from school, no books or notebooks I can see, just a guitar riding up and down his back every step he takes, and he's holding hands with Elma's granddaughter—I don't want to think what else they do.

One time poor Jack and me were at the Saint Theresa's picnic. I was maybe old as Sissie. "Come on and see my car," he says to me. He gets behind the wheel and I climb in beside him, my heart is thumping. He takes my hand. I don't know where to put my eyes. Then he lifts my hand, lays it on my lap and presses. The sweetness that came over me. It was the first time, and—to tell God's truth—better than anything my Al ever made me feel. But wasn't I the baby? I began to cry. He got scared, I guess. "Let's go back," he says, hobbles off, and leaves me there. Never asked me to sit with him again. If I was one of these girls today like you see in tight pants and showing off their flesh, I wouldn't wait for an invite. Bold things.

Then there's young Penny, from the two-bedroom bungalow up the hill. Comes by pushing the twins and looking like number three is on the way and—what I hear—her husband still just pumping gas and changing tires at a place out on the highway. And most days Maggie, stucco house on the corner, comes stomping by, mad at the world 'cause her postman husband moved in with some blondie lives on his route. Lots of others parading down the sidewalk. Some I know by name, some just by face, once in a while a stranger.

And naturally, all day long, except when I go in at noon to fix a tuna sandwich and bring it out with me or when I pay a visit to the powder room, I can't help seeing what's going on with the Koreans across the street. Truth is, they're pretty quiet—even when the two boys come out to play, they just toss a rubber ball and, if they talk, they keep it down. Nang, the mother's name is. One day she caught me sweeping my front walk and asked me over for a cup of tea. I told her, "Thank you, no." Nang, she said, or maybe Nam. I don't know what the husband or the kids are called. At night, I can look straight into their living room and see the TV on. They watch the news and all, just like Americans.

Sissie's in her kitchen now. Must have come in when I wasn't looking. What's she after? She's pulling a quart of ice cream from the freezer, hugging it against her waist, prying off the lid. She's got it off, and now she's licking it. That gal's got more bad habits. Now she's digging in with what looks to be a serving spoon. Don't try to put the whole thing in your mouth, you goose. Makes my teeth ache to watch her. There she goes, taking the carton into another room, doesn't care it's gonna drip down her sweater or on the rug. She's thirteen. Runs and skates and rides her bike, but too weak to get a little bowl down from the shelf. Kids.

Across from Sissie's is the Filipino couple. They moved in first, then the Koreans. Next thing, I suppose, the street will be nothing but these people. All the good old Irish and German families packing up and moving out. I got nothing against the Orientals—they keep their yards up nice—but I don't want to be a minority on my own street and have foreigners staring at me like I'm a freak.

Next door to me, in the two-family on the left, used to be the Muellers on top and the Mahoneys underneath. Now, up and down, it's a passel of young people—I'd say in their twenties—boys and girls together, all helter-skelter. Even, one of them is colored. I started out trying to keep track who's who, but it's not easy when one or the other keeps disappearing and someone new keeps popping up. Which isn't right. Newcomers got a duty to make themselves known—say here I am and this one's my brother and this one's my mother and we don't make trouble.

On the other side, I got my Arabs.

"I'd be scared," my sister Tillie says. But it's just Sissie's family, three grown-ups and three kids. They been there upwards of ten years already, and I'm kind of used to them. Seasons it's too cold for the porch, I sit here like today and watch them from my living room, they keep me entertained. Nothing but a narrow driveway and a scraggly hedge between my house and them. "Cheek and jowl," her uncle tells me. "So be good," he says. Imagine saying that to me! *I'll cheek you*, I think. He's got his better points, though. Since my Al passed on, he mows my backyard and the little patch in front. Likes the exercise, he says. Still, I don't want to be beholden. So when I hear the mower, I take him out a plate of my divinity with pecans—to that he won't say no—enough for him and the whole crew at home.

Their kitchen is right opposite my chair. At night, I lift a slat on my venetian blind and take a gander. I could tell you if they're having regular or funny food for supper and who's missing from the table and who washes up. Afterwards, the grown-ups sit around, swilling down coffee and smoking 'til you can bet the air's not fit to breathe. No mystery where Sissie got that filthy habit from. And, of course, they're yakking to beat the band, laughing, throwing out their arms, leaning into each other's faces. I wonder sometimes, what gets them so worked up.

"They must be hatching something," Tillie said last week. She was calling on the phone from L.A., where her house is.

"Like what?" I said.

"Don't you watch the news?" So I knew she was remembering. And that made me remember, too. Poor souls calling home to say good-bye forever on their cell phones and the ones the TV showed, dropping from the sky. It made my stomach drop to watch them. And then the towers sliding to the street like someone kicked them in the gut, coughing up smoke and dirt and ashes, the air thick like stew. I watched the people running, and I could hardly catch my breath—looking back and running like King

Kong was after them. Wicked, wicked what those Arabs did. I'm glad they died. But I couldn't make it fit with the folks next door. Hard to picture Sissie and them praying like you see—stretching and bending double with their fannies in the air. I'd be surprised.

"They're not Arabs through and through," I told her. "The mother doesn't cover up, maybe just a scarf around her hair. And no beards on the men excepting Sunday when they don't bother shaving. Unless you want to count that little line of mustache on the uncle's lip."

"That shows they're crafty," Tillie said. "They want to melt right in."

Younger than me, but she's Miss Know-It-All. I switched the phone from one ear to the other.

"That so?"

1:00 P.M.

Well, something's fishy in the state of Denmark. I was at the sink, peeling hard-boiled eggs, when the doorbell rings. Which is unusual. Hardly anybody drops in these days except the gal who goes downstairs to read the water meter. I dried my hands on one of the twin towels I keep hanging by the sink and went to answer. It's Sissie with her nose against the window pane in my front door, and her hands around her eyes, trying to see in. When she spots me coming, she gives a little wave. By the time I notice someone's with her, it's too late to lay low in the kitchen and make out I'm not at home. I don't like strangers on my porch. Even Sissie, I prefer her at a distance.

When I unchained the door and pulled it part way, I got a better look. The boy had a head of black curls and was maybe seventeen, too old for her to pal around with. And no jacket on—just a quilted vest over a long-sleeved jersey. You know the type, too tough to feel the cold.

"Meet my cousin Mo," she said.

"Mo, short for what?" I said. I spoke right up. I didn't want him to think I was afraid, just 'cause he was six feet and shoulders on him like man.

He grinned down at me like he knew me all my life. "Mohammed," he said, which made me jump. Sissie giggled. Up close I saw the white stuff she puts on her pimples to dry them out.

"Can he use your bathroom?" Sissie said. Just like that, as if it was nothing she was asking. What would you have done? Myself, I folded my arms and looked her in the eye, waiting for it to dawn she was out of line. I'll tell you what. I don't believe in coming right out and saying no to people. Why get a person mad and looking to do you a bad turn? Besides, what if I need Sissie's help some day to scare away a burglar? Or to pick up milk or a loaf of rye from the corner store when time comes I find it hard to walk there in the winter. You gotta think ahead.

"He needs to go real bad." Sissie poked him in the ribs. "Tell her," she said. He gave her a little push back, but he still had his eyes on me. Dark brown with long black lashes.

"What's wrong with your bathroom?" I said to her, wondering what was going on.

"I locked myself out of the house again."

"Duh!" the boy said.

"Duh!" she said and made her face into a silly mask, her eyes crossed, her tongue falling out of the corner of her mouth.

I was stuck. I mean I couldn't tell him, "Go do it in her yard." And all the other houses, the people at work, the kids in school, which is where these two characters should have been. So I opened the door enough to let them in one at a time. Then I pointed the boy to where the downstairs bathroom is. "Nothing in there to steal," I told myself. But how did I know he was clean and didn't have some disease? I just hoped he wouldn't make a stink.

While he's in there, Sissie's making herself at home at my kitchen table.

"No school today?" I say.

"No heat in the building"—she hunched her shoulders in her parka and made like she was shivering—"they sent us home." That was nothing but a lie because, if it was true, why sneak around? So that was strike two against her—first she brings this boy with muscles and eyelashes into my house and now she's fibbing in my face. Strike three if you count her playing hooky though that wasn't something aimed at me.

"Can I have a glass of water?" she says.

I look at her hard. "Do you think that's a good idea?"

"I'm thirsty."

"But it'll make you want to go." The things you have to tell these kids.

And now I'm getting worried Mo's taking too long in there. Drugs, I think. I picture him sticking a needle in his arm or using my own drinking glass to wash down pills. Or could be he was already drugged up when he came and now he's passed out on my clean floor and maybe cracked his head against the tub. Blood on my white tile, the thought makes me feel sick. "Go get him," I say.

"What? No way," Sissie says, getting ready to giggle again, but I cut her short.

"Just give a knock and say it's getting late."

She jumped up. "I'll tell him you want to pee."

"You'll do no such thing! Go on now, get him out."

2:30 P.M.

My own bathroom, but I didn't feel easy going in after that boy was there. I paced a bit outside the door, then I faced up to it. Got out the brush, squirted toilet cleaner in the bowl, and scrubbed. Next I put on rubber gloves and went over the rest of the commode with Lysol and paper towels. Then I did the floor and tore off and threw away about a yard of toilet paper because you never know. When I was done, I took my drinking glass and put it in the dishwasher and threw out the gloves—not cheap ones, either—in the garbage can outside. Back in the house, I looked around some more, thinking if there was something I forgot. The toilet brush. I stuck it in a plastic bag and poked it in the barrel with the gloves. Gloves gone, brush gone—that boy, he might just as well have picked my pocket. But, at least now, when nature calls, I can go about my business without worrying.

After all that, I'm late getting at my lunch. But everything's ready now, set out on the card table in the living room, right by the window. Egg salad on white today, sliced tomato with mayonnaise, celery for my veggie, a cup of decaf and, for dessert, two chocolate cupcakes with fudge frosting. When Tillie nags about cholesterol and such, I talk right over her. "Thank you," I say, "I eat very well."

Uh-oh, I spot some action. Next door Sissie and Mo are climbed up on the bulkhead of the house and working at the back window, except they keep having to quit when they start laughing hard and bumping elbows. I wonder if I should rap on my windowpane and let them know I found it in a corner of the bathroom, behind the door. It's his, of course. I guess I know what belongs in my own bathroom and what doesn't. Tiny little oval thing. Like a girl's charm almost, but wood around the edge and in the middle a stone painted like an eye. A blue eye, if you please. I looked down when I was cleaning and caught it looking up at me. I didn't want to touch the thing, and I didn't feel exactly right about scooping it in the dustpan and throwing it away. So it's still sitting there. Except I dropped a square of bathroom tissue on it. Call me crazy, but I don't want that eyeball staring at me when I'm pulling down my underwear.

Now I see they got the window jimmied open and Sissie's climbing in headfirst, her legs sticking in the air. Praise heaven, she wears jeans and not a skirt. Mo's grabbed her feet and he's pushing her like a wheelbarrow. Now there he goes, diving through the window, too. Must have landed right on top of her. He didn't have to do that. She says he's her cousin, but I don't know. Well, not my business, is it? I'm not her mother. Al and me, we wanted kids, but it wasn't in the cards. At least, I wanted them. Truth is I don't think he cared. Men. Except at the end, when he knew he was going, he felt he'd missed out. It used to make me sad—no kids, I mean—but look at youngsters today. Sometimes I talk to Al in my head. "Could be we were better off." And, anyway, I tell him, in the end kids go off and leave you on your own. "Not in my country," Sissie's uncle says. Big talk.

3:30 P.M.

It's quiet now. But half hour ago, I was in the kitchen washing up my lunch things when the doorbell rings again. This time there's three of them. Sissie, Mo, and another boy a couple inches shorter and a little younger, but same flashing eyes, same hair, same looking like he knows something I don't and he's gonna keep it to himself. Not to mention, same no scarf or hat or jacket. I looked him in the eye. "You'll catch your death," I said. He ducked his head so I could hardly see his face.

"This is Mo's brother," Sissie says. "You can call him Freddie." She means like I call her "Sissie." Not her real name, which I can't get my tongue around, but "close enough," her uncle says.

"Mo lost something," she tells me. "He thinks maybe in your house."

"Bathroom," I say. "I haven't touched it. You boys stay put. Sissie, you come on with me." But, of course, all three of them traipsed after. Deaf.

I went in first, Sissie and Mo squeezed in behind.

I pointed. "There it is."

"Where?" she said.

"There, under the tissue."

She looked at Mo, and he looked at me.

"Do you want trouble?" he said. "You asking for it, you'll get it."

I put my hand to my throat. What kind of thing was that to

say? And his crony waiting outside the door. "You should thank me," I said. "Keeping it nice for you. Someone else would have chucked it in the trash."

"It's bad luck," Sissie said.

"What's bad luck?"

"What you did. That there's a thing to protect against the evil eye."

"And what might that be?"

"When some people look at you, their eyes can dry up your blood or suck out your brains."

"Sissie," I said, "Don't be so ignorant, a big girl like you."

"It's true. Uncle says no, but I'm sure that's how my grandfather, my *jiddu*, died."

"And what good's this little trinket going to do you?"

Sissie sighed like she thought I was being dumb on purpose. "Everybody knows," she said, "evil eye is blue, that's why you need another blue eye to fight back at it."

I wanted to get in my two cents then but do you think she'd let me? "You covered it up," she says, "so it can't see what's coming. And, what's worse, looks like you're bragging you don't need it."

She was giving me the creeps. "Stuff and nonsense," I said. "You're talking crazy."

"You'll see," she said and goes back to staring at the floor.

All this time Mo's waiting. Now he knelt down and pulled away the tissue and rubbed the charm against his jeans. Then he stood up, kissed it, and put in his pocket. "Dumb broad," he said.

Sissie whacked him in the arm. "Shut up," she said. And then she says to me, "He didn't mean it. Boys got no manners."

Mo was staring at me. "You got blue eyes."

"Grey. My sister Tillie is the lucky one got the baby blues."

"Yours look blue to me."

"So what?" Sissie was standing up for me. "She's my neighbor. Now say you're sorry."

"Yeah," he says. "Okay."

4:00 P.M.

This time of day I should be watching Oprah and putting potatoes on to boil, not passing by the window every chance, to see what I can see. Sissie's on my mind. Alone with those boys, says they're her cousins. Maybe yes, maybe no. It's well known I'm not the kind to poke my nose in other people's business. But if she was mine, I'd be tickled a neighbor was looking out for her. I'd say thank you if the neighbor was to call her on the phone or even take a chance of catching cold by running over to say, "What the devil's going on?"

4:30 P.M.

Every ten minutes by my watch, I've been dialing. When Sissie answers, I hang up. Just making sure she's not laying on her back—saints forgive me for what I'm thinking—that big fellow over her, and the brother standing watch. But just now, when I cradled the receiver and went to take another look, Mo gave me such a start. Big as life, he's staring at me from Sissie's kitchen window. The eyes on him. He held his hand up in a fist and banged against the pane. Threatening me, who never did a thing against him and even let him use my toilet. Like my Al used to say, sometimes it doesn't pay to do a kindness.

I should have run into another room. Instead, I sat down fast and pulled back in my barrel chair to where I hoped Mo couldn't see me. My face was burning and my heart was racing like I was going through the change again. Something not right about that boy, I knew it from the git-go. So here I'm sitting like a statue. Don't dare stir a muscle, much less roll my head around to peek.

Pretty soon, though, Sissie's mother will be pulling in the driveway. She'll shoo Mo off. "Go watch TV," she'll say, "let me get supper on." And later, if he tries to tell on me, the uncle will say not to bother an old lady living all alone. Unless, of course, what I suspect, Mo's not their family and got not business being there at all. In which case, he'll be clearing out, him and his buddy. Please, God, don't let them come near me.

5:00 P.M.

When it got dark enough Mo couldn't see in, I came out from hiding. No lights on in their kitchen either, so I couldn't tell if he was still standing there or not. I felt my way, checking all the first floor windows. The front door's always locked and so's the back. And the door that takes a person to the cellar, I made sure of that. In the kitchen, I yanked down the blinds plus the one on the little window in the pantry. Last thing, I shut the door into the hall and the swinging one into the living room. That door, I used to think it was a no-good nuisance. Just goes to show. Last thing, I reached up for the crocheted pull hanging from the fluorescent fixture in the ceiling. It's my house, I'm not going to sit here in the dark.

Haven't got the heart to fix a proper dinner, but if I get hungry, there's milk and eggs in the fridge, a couple oranges, a head of lettuce, and some left-over tuna. Not to mention a slab of chocolate layer cake sitting on the counter. If I have to relieve myself, the downstairs bathroom is just a step away. All in all, I can hold out easy. Best of all, I got a wall phone handy, and I can grab it if I hear a noise. Of course, these days who would I call? It's not the same as when the Muellers and the Mahoneys lived next door. Now seems there's only strangers every side of me. Still, a telephone's a comfort. Truth to tell, it was Tillie said no kitchen should be without one. Sometimes she's right.

But, oh, it makes me sad. I used to think if I was ever in a fix and had to, I could call Sissie's family for help. "Don't hesitate," her uncle told me. Now I'm wondering if he'll ever even mow my lawn again.

5:10 P.M.

Mother of God, there goes the phone.

5:30 P.M.

I wasn't going to answer except it was Friday, and that's the day Tillie likes to call. "Hello," I says. "Hello?" I hear two people arguing on the other end. Then it's Sissie's voice telling me, "Poor Freddie's sick." More arguing. Then Mo gets on. "Lady, take off the curse." And then—listen to this—he says, "Or else."

My hand was trembling so, I could hardly hook the phone back on the jack.

When Tillie heard my voice, I could tell it took her by surprise. "Why don't you use your head," she says, "and wait until the rates go down all the way before you phone?" And then she got suspicious. "Why you calling, anyway? What's wrong?"

"My neighbors."

"The terrorists?"

"Yeah," I said, not to put too fine a point on it. "They're spying on the house and yelling at me on the telephone."

"Didn't I tell you? You better call the cops. Go on, hang up and do it now."

"It's only one of them. He's got black eyes."

"Never mind his eyes. What if he's got a bomb?"

6:30 P.M.

I dialed 911, they're going to send around a cruiser. I'm wondering now if I did right. Flashing lights outside my home, the whole street looking out its windows, phoning house to house to ask what's going on. Tomorrow, on their way to work, folks staring. And not one bit of all this mess my fault.

But when the cops show, naturally I won't lie. I'll have to point them to the house next door and tell them about the boys with scary eyes that Sissie's family is harboring. I'll fill them in what happened—the banging on the window, the staring in at me, the threats. They'll see how I live alone and need protection. They'll give those folks a talking to. "We're going to keep our eye on you"—that's what they'll say—"so just be good and watch your step."

Stupid, though, hiding in my kitchen, like I'm the criminal. Guess I can walk into my own living room. Guess I can look out my window if I've a mind to.

Lights on now across the way. There's Mo, front and center. Must be, after all, he's really kin. He's hanging something tiny on the window—probably more of that hocus-pocus Sissie was going on about. Okay you, now move away. But he just stands there like a sentry, looking out. Hope he likes looking at his own reflection 'cause he may be facing me but I'm betting himself is all that he can see. Behind him, the whole bunch is gathered 'round the table, dad and mama, kids and uncle. Freddie, too, so how sick can he be? They're all just as usual—talking, laughing, passing dishes.

Never dreaming what's gonna hit.

Let's Dance

"I've got this rule, smartie: if you threaten to push me out an up-stairs window, you can't stay in my house." Dottie was at the sink, scouring shreds of burnt egg from an iron frying pan. "So run along."

Nadia glared at her mother's back. "Right. Like where am I supposed to go?"

"Try your math teacher, she gave you an A."

"B plus, you never get things straight." Nadia paced in her beach thongs from fridge to screen door and back again. "Anyway, I didn't say I *would* push you, I said you make me so mad I *could* push you. There's a difference."

"Not to me."

Nadia watched her mother peck at a last little bit on the inside of the frying pan. Not like her to be so fussy, she must be really mad.

"Okay, I'm sorry."

Dottie turned, the scouring pad in her hand, water dripping down her wrist. "And wishing me a broken leg? Nice talk!"

Nadia smiled.

"Oh, I see you like the idea."

"Gee, Mom, can't you take a joke?"

"Some joke." She turned back to the sink. "Are you really sorry?"

Nadia moved in to hug her mother around the waist. "Yes."

Dottie shook her head. "I don't know." She reached up and ran wet fingers across her daughter's cheek. "My baby, the terrorist."

Nadia pulled away and gave her mother a little smack on the behind. "Don't start."

Nadia's father was Arab, that was the point. A real Arab born overseas. Nabil had come to America to study, found a job, then sent for others in his family. By the time Dottie met and married him, he was a package deal—mother, father, cousins, Eastern church. Dottie was "mongrel American Protestant," that's what she called herself. Nothing to merit a second glance.

Since she couldn't compete, she'd gone all out to blur the line between her husband's family and herself. Dottie had learned to scoop out marrow squash, puree chickpeas, and stuff a capon with rice and lamb. She'd picked up courtesy phrases—*alhamdillah* when her in-laws politely hoped that she was well, *tfaddalu* when she ushered them into the dining room for Sunday dinner. She'd even joined her husband's church and tried not to gawk at priests dressed like women in long brocaded vestments and at the icons, flat as a child's drawing; and not to sway when censors swung in her direction, fogging the air she breathed, making her head spin. At the wedding they'd circled the ceremonial table, hand in hand with their attendants, her gold foil crown attached to his by a silk ribbon. To Dottie, it hadn't felt like church at all, more like playing at dress up or like singing the lead, as she used to, in high school musicals. She liked performing.

After the divorce, she left the church, or it left her. Looking back, she was never sure. But she knew why she'd walked out on her husband. "Boring," she'd explain. What she meant was "not exotic." His dark eyes and thick black hair, even his dusky church, a form of false advertising. "Bait and switch" a friend suggested. After that, Dottie had used the phrase herself, pleased when it got a laugh. Once she forgot and said it in front of Nadia, who'd stormed off to her bedroom and slammed the door.

Her husband's parents were a different matter. When their path crossed Dottie's at the market or the bank, she still kissed them on both cheeks, called them "Mom" and "Dad," wanted them to find her charming. Immigrants, shy and unsure, they didn't have it in them to be rude to this blond American whose English cavorted like a TV jingle. "Keep the peace," they told each other. "For the sake of the little girl." One day, running into them on the sidewalk outside the elementary school, Dottie broke her news. She and Nadia were moving to a darling town on Cape Cod in Massachusetts. "It's like a postcard," she said, "sand dunes and cranberry bogs and shops that sell painted rockers and wreaths made out of seashells. I'll send you one for Christmas."

"So far away?" her father-in-law said. The muscles around her mother-in-law's sweet mouth went hard.

"Oh, it's not far at all. Four hours by car." She would not be put in the wrong. "You'll come visit all the time." She wagged her finger like a toy metronome—"Don't forget to bring your swimsuits."

In Orleans, they rented a cottage that had begun life as a hunter's camp but had long since turned domestic—two bedrooms, an upstairs loft, a kitchen with built-in dishwasher and microwave. All summer the woods in which it sat offered shade on shade—"No use trying to plant," Dottie told Nadia, who'd had visions of towering sunflowers and pink roses like those she'd seen climbing stone walls along Cape roads. Later, when the scrub oaks shrugged off their leaves, Lake Pearl surprised them through the branches, skaters on its back, and now and then a bearded man fishing through the ice. "He's back," Dottie would call out, or Nadia would if she spotted him first.

Dottie settled in to keeping the books and part-time clerking at the local Army-Navy Store. "You should see the people with money come in," she told Nadia. "Counting their pennies, that's how they get rich." On days off, she took Nadia miniature golfing or to an early movie; after supper, when she could find a sitter, she stepped out to dance. Open-mike nights at the local club, she put on her clingiest outfit and sweet talked the emcee into letting her belt out a tune at precisely ten fifteen. "My birthday," she told him, and when he didn't understand, she wrote it on a paper place mat—"10/15." The two of them wound up in bed.

Men came and went while she waited for the love of her life to make himself known. No rush, she thought, except when something like Nadia getting her first period reminded her that time was passing. Or the night Nadia came home smashed from a party. The boy who'd driven her and helped her in the house turned red when he spotted Dottie stretched out on the sofa in a black negligee that had fallen open. It was so cute, Dottie thought, the way he hadn't known where to put his eyes. Their fight the next morning was what had led to Nadia's vision of her mother flying out the window.

Nabil had lost no time remarrying—this time a younger girl from his parents' village—and moved with her to southern California, where he became a partner in his cousin's import-export business. After months of urging on the telephone— "Baba, Mama, you will swear you are in Lebanon. Come. Let the sun warm your bones"—his parents followed, moving in with their bedroom set and shirt boxes full of photos, making themselves at home as they never could have under Dottie's roof. A continent now between Nadia and her Arab family.

Occasionally, her father came East. But, for three weeks every summer and then on Thanksgiving or Christmas break, it was her turn to visit. When Nabil led her through the doorway, her *jiddu,* who'd been pacing downstairs all morning, would take her in his arms and kiss her head. Then, his hand not letting go of hers, grope for a folded square of handkerchief in his jacket pocket. Her *sittu,* soft to the touch and plump, would sit beside her on the sofa, smoothing back Nadia's straight, fine hair, laying her head on Nadia's shoulder, whispering in Arabic—"My heart, may you bury me." Nadia's father translated. "She's wishing you long life."

Her stepmother, not to be outdone, prepared a feast each evening. Rolled grape leaves one day, then stuffed eggplant in tomato sauce with pine nuts, then lamb with artichoke, and so on; for dessert, sticky pastries stuffed with white cheese, walnuts, or pistachios. She tried not to be hurt when Nadia mentioned that her mother knew how to cook and bake the same. Her half-brother and sister stared when she arrived and then forgot about her. She had no way with younger children, no games or silly jokes or stories to cast her as a favorite.

Once each summer, her father took her for a morning drive

through Beverly Hills and on up to Palisades Park. As they walked the cliffs, he quizzed her on her schoolwork and on her mother's boyfriends and, one year, on her teeth. "If you neglect them, you'll be sorry." She was staring out over the water, trying to make out Catalina Island in the distance, and didn't answer. He touched her hand. *"Ya, baba, sma'i minni."* Then, remembering the sad fact that she didn't know a word of Arabic, except for foods and for curses Dottie had held on to, he'd translate. "Take my advice." *In English,* he thought, *the words are cold.*

The summer excursion before her senior year, his face was serious.

"Big decisions coming up," he said. "What's on the agenda after graduation?"

"I'll do something. College, I guess."

"College, yes. I suggest engineering." He thought a moment. "Nothing wrong with business, either."

Winding home along Sunset Boulevard, Nadia chattered on about her best friend—she was an identical twin but much nicer on the inside than her sister—"isn't that weird?" And about their little brother, who had a port wine birthmark on his cheek—"good thing he's not a girl." And about Betsy, her toy schnauzer who had run away—"if she was dead, I'd know it." She didn't bring up boys, and he didn't ask. "The mother's job," he told his wife.

"How was it?" Dottie asked when she picked her up at Logan.

"Good. Everyone says hi."

"Everyone?"

"I didn't take a poll."

It *had* been good, like Disney World or summer camp. But, even though she knew they loved her—her grandparents, for sure—those people in California were finally only characters in a book. When she looked back after going through security at the airport and saw her *jiddu* blowing his nose, her *sittu* in a flowered dress, hugging her black purse against her chest, the others to one side, their hands making little rubbings in the air that passed for goodbye waves, she threw a kiss, turned, and it was like closing the cover of the book and putting it away.

By the time next June rolled around, a lot had happened. Nadia was accepted at a community college. Her father wrote his delight, passing on her grandparents' blessings and a list of people Nadia had never heard of that they'd telephoned the news to. "Jeesh," she said, "it's not like Harvard wants me." Dottie got married. "What took you so long to track me down?" she teased, whether they were in bed together—he'd moved in—or out to dinner with the gang. Mr. Right was thirty, twelve years her junior—she was glad to show Nabil he wasn't the only one could baby-snatch. His name was Ezra and he was Jewish. She'd like to see Nabil's face when he heard that.

"Jews are an intelligent race," she told Nadia. It was Sunday afternoon, Ezra off somewhere, Dottie lounging on the sofa in bare feet, a *TV Guide* splayed open on her tummy. Nadia was curled up in an easy chair, leafing through the text of her biology assignment.

"Oh, I'm not talking business smarts though they got that, all right. I'm talking books and professors and philosophers and, of course, you've heard of Einstein. It's well known, that's what makes them sexy. When the brain's in tip-top condition, so's the rest of the machinery."

Nadia was studying an illustration of the human male. "What?"

"Yes, yes. Look at that Kissinger, ugly as sin, but the brain on him. Dating movie stars half his age."

"He's got all those chins."

"Never mind, it must be he can still do his duty." Dottie yawned and stretched, reaching for the ceiling. "Naturally, with Ezra I have no complaints in that department. But he's another thinker, a professional man." Ezra owned a pharmacy. "You should hear the stories. Let's just say if it wasn't for his sharp eye, a lot of folks on the lower Cape would be dead today or have bum livers from the mistakes these high-and-mighty doctors make. And, Nadia baby"—she wrapped her arms around her knees—"won't it be handy to have someone in the house to tell us what to take for cramps or if we get the flu?"

"I don't get the flu." Nadia shut her textbook. She'd find fifteen minutes in the morning to run through her assignment.

Dottie had decided to convert. "Ezra thinks it's better that way. One flesh, one faith, he says. Isn't that pretty?" She'd taken classes with a rabbi in town and memorized enough to answer softball questions. One thing she had her heart set on was a *mikveh*, the convert's ritual immersion in a pool of water. Of course, it would be only women watching—"praise God for small mercies," she told Nadia. Ezra and his closest buddies would wait outside the door while the waters warmed her naked body. As it happened, Nadia was being a good sport, brushing out her mother's hair. Dottie stopped her hand in mid-stroke. "Those guys"—Dottie winked at her in the mirror—"I guess their imaginations will be working overtime."

"I guess." Nadia laid down her brush and started in massaging Dottie's shoulders.

Dottie breathed a deep sigh. "And know what else I'm think-ing? I have a bat mitzvah for myself in mind. Remember Ezra's cousin—what's her name—last month? I think I'd carry it off pretty well. Better than her anyways, the way she mumbled. That's where my stage experience will help."

"Don't you think you're overdoing it?"

Dottie shook her head. "No such thing as overdo." Dottie had a list like that. "No such thing as too sexy." "No such thing as too much chocolate."

Nadia let it go. Why should she care, as long as she didn't have to get up there with her? When Ezra heard, he said, "Sure. But you know it means two years of Hebrew lessons." Nadia could see that was the end of that.

Dottie had her *mikveh* on a Friday. On Monday, Nadia met Nick. It was the first day of a history class, and the instructor, a fiftyish woman with frizzy hair and wooden beads cascading from her earlobes, was asking the students to introduce themselves. "We're going to be a team," she said. "I want you to know each other's names and some one thing about each person." Ten min-utes into the period, she rested her knuckles on a front-row desk.

"Class, here's a young man from overseas. Nick, please tell us about yourself."

The other students were mostly leaning on their elbows or slouched in their seats, staring at their desks. Nick stood, looked around, and made what amounted to a little bow. "First, I ask please to forgive my accent."

The teacher, lowered her eyelids and shook her head. Her ear-rings kicked up their heels. "Nonsense, your English is just fine."

Nadia waited. He was unlike any boy she'd ever met. No one

would call him handsome. His ears stuck out, a front tooth was crooked. But he was classy (her mother's word came to her out of nowhere), the way he held himself and smiled and moved his head. What smarter, richer world did he come out of? Nadia wanted to wrap one of his dark curls around her finger, she wanted to squeeze his slim hands with her own. She wanted whatever he had to rub off on her.

"I am Greek," he said. "From Cyprus. My family, we moved ourselves to the States last year."

The teacher nodded. "And your plans for the future?"

"I hope to become a filmmaker."

"How wonderful. Isn't that wonderful, class?" She looked at them reproachfully, her would-be accountants and computer programmers. "An artist in our midst."

Nick flushed. Behind him, classmates were exchanging glances.

Nadia was up next. "I'm Arab." It was a sentence she'd never said before in her whole life. A spur-of-the-moment gift to Nick, a leap like a ballerina's—that's how she pictured it—lofting her to where he stood alone on the other side of an invisible hedge. Leaving behind that shadowy classroom of losers. Her desk was just behind his, and, as she spoke, he shifted around to face her. She smiled and inched her hands along her desk in his direction. She hoped he'd see that she was different.

For the rest of the class period, Nadia plotted—on the way out, she'd drop her books and, when he stopped to help her, she'd say something funny about the teacher's earrings. One thing would lead to another. But, in the end, he beat her to the punch.

"Would you like to drink a coffee?" They took their cups to a table by a window in the caf. "In Cyprus, some people, they say bad things about the Arabs. I think it is the same thing here?"

"People are dumb."

"They say things to hurt you?"

Nadia's mind raced, ransacking memories.

"Once someone called me a terrorist."

Nick shook his head.

"I can't talk about it," she said.

"Of course." He lifted his coffee mug—Nadia like the way he wrapped both hands around it. "Nadia, you told the professor you dream to travel around the world?"

"Yes, like you."

Nick laughed. "But I have seen little, perhaps you will take me with you. But I am selfish. You will go, a free woman on your own, and then come home to Cape Cod and tell me everything."

"I'll take a camera."

"No, I prefer to hear the stories in your words. You must keep a diary."

"It's funny you say that. I've been thinking I might go in for journalism."

"But this is fantastic."

With him across from her and the sun warm on her face, it was easier than she would have thought to re-create herself.

"Do you know," he said, "what I tell them in Cyprus?"

She shook her head.

"I tell them Arabs and Cypriots are cousins—even our super-stitions are the same—black birds, they predict death, the evil eye gives sickness to a child. Yes, we are very close."

.   .   .

From the start, Dottie took a dislike to Nick. The church, his church, was part of it. Orthodox, same as Nabil's, the one she'd been married in.

"Hello?" Nadia said, not bothering to turn around. She was at the kitchen counter, slicing banana into a bowl of Cheerios; Dottie was at the butcher-block table that looked out toward the lake, spooning sugar into her coffee mug. Only the two of them, Ezra gone to the pharmacy, the radio off now.

"Just because it didn't work out with you and Dad, doesn't mean I can never be friends with anyone in that religion." She reached for the milk, blinking as she looked up into a narrow shaft of sunlight through the window.

Dottie dipped again into the sugar bowl. "What do you mean 'friends'?"

Nadia didn't answer. She was stooped over the sink, making short work of her cereal.

Dottie tasted her coffee and frowned. "You know they treat women terrible."

"Who do?"

"Them, them. Your Orthodox. Almost bad as the Mohammedans."

"Muslims." Nadia might not get all A's in school, but she knew that much.

"Don't be smart."

Nadia glanced at the wall clock—salvaged from a grade school classroom—took a final mouthful and a last sip of apple juice, then gave a quick rinse to her breakfast things.

"Those Mooslims," Dottie said. "They make the women dress like witches, all in black and cover up their arms and legs and half their faces." She looked Nadia up and down, bare midriff and a glimpse of cleavage. "They won't have you, I can tell you that."

"Are you nuts? What's that got to do with Nick?"

"At least Jews have women rabbis." Dottie gave a little sniff. "We're not backward."

Nadia started out the door.

"Where you going?"

"Mall."

"I bet." But Dottie was wrong. Nadia wasn't lying.

Around one, Ezra came home for lunch, and Dottie started in, what she'd said, what Nadia had said and how she'd said it.

"Can't you just leave her be?" He was bored with the subject.

"I tell you, Ezra, it's serious. I don't know where or when, but, sure as I'm standing here, they're doing it."

"Show me." Ezra reached out and pulled his wife in hard against his chest.

"Okay, lover"—her voice was deep in her throat—"step one."

"Your mother. . . ," Nick began. They were strolling through the mini-mall, sometimes holding hands, sometimes one pacing in a circle while the other hung back to study a display of digital gadgets, electric guitars, or silver earrings. When Nadia heard "mother," she pulled up short.

"What's wrong?" she said.

"Nothing is wrong." He smiled broadly. "All things are right. Your mother—I meant only to say—she has *joie de vivre,* she's full of life."

"Oh, yeah, she's something else." Nadia made a face, slipped her hand in Nick's, and started walking.

"Explain please?"

"You know—she's too much."

"But this is good?"

"Well,"—Nadia thought it over—"she's not boring."

"Exactly as I said."

Nadia frowned. "She's got her faults."

Thanksgiving weekend, her father and his SUV were there to meet them at the airport. Not that he approved. And not that he wasn't worried about his younger children. What would they think, seeing their sister traveling across country with a man? All right, a boy. Worse, when you came to it. He remembered his own fierce adolescent urges. How could Dottie allow it? Didn't she care about the family's good name? At first, when Dottie left him, he was more hurt than anybody knew. And, even after he'd remarried, he missed her quick step on the stairs, her unexpected impulses, her playfulness in bed. But with the years he came to see he'd had a close escape. And now—well, he'd always known daughters were trouble in the making.

It had started with Nick's saying, "I will miss you."

"Oh, me too."

They were in a diner on Main Street, eating bowls of chili, munching on tortilla chips and sipping lemonades. Through the picture window, they watched the rain. A dismal early November downpour. Nadia touched his hand, he turned his head.

"Come with me," she said.

"I can't. My family, my mother." It was an unanswerable argument. But she wasn't giving up.

"Friday, then. We'll go out together early Friday and come back on Sunday night."

"Yes?"

"Yes!"

"But the ticket."

They pooled their resources. Half from money her father had given her last summer, the rest he'd earned delivering a local weekly aimed at tourists.

Dottie didn't fight it. "Go, go. We'll just see what your father has to say."

"That's a new one," Nadia told Nick.

"Every family," he said, "they have their own ways."

Nadia wasn't clear what she was expecting from these two days and nights. Despite Dottie's suspicions, she and Nick had never been to bed except in Nadia's imagination. And, she liked to think, in his. Until they met, she'd been what her girlfriends called "a practicing virgin," someone who'd tried sex once or twice and been in no hurry to go through that again. In any case, her father's house, inhabited by three generations, was no place for experiment.

So it wasn't big-time sex on the agenda. But it was something. A point to be made, she sensed. But what? "That I'm really Arab" was the best she could come up with. Nick would hear her grandparents' accents, their stories about the village, the homesickness in their voices. That edge of sadness had always hurt Nadia, as if it were a door closed in her face. But now it would weigh in her favor—like a credential on an application. Evidence that she and Nick, the immigrant boy, belonged together. That no girl in their class or in the school or that he might meet on the beach next summer could understand him so well.

After embracing their granddaughter, they turned, eyes still moist, to her young man. *Ahlan wa sahlan,* they repeated. "Welcome, welcome to our home." *Sittu*, who'd changed out of her housedress, could not stop smiling. *Jiddu*, in a white shirt that looked to be new, held out his hand. This was more like it. Her father hadn't been out-and-out rude on the drive home, but he'd acted as if his mind was elsewhere. Nadia had tried to cover up by laughing a lot and going on about any odd thing that popped into her head. She was angry. In front of Nick, her father had made her take center stage and, of course, she'd come out sounding stupid.

That evening, Nadia's stepmother went all out. Brown lentil soup with lemon, sole layered in a garlic and tahini sauce, salad of tender baby okra, and—something even Dottie had never attempted—home-baked Syrian bread. She tossed four rounds of dough on a flat stone in a good hot oven. Through the glass window, Nadia and Nick watched the loaves puff into pockets. "You see, is miracle," her stepmother said. "Up, up"—she lifted her hands, coaxing the bread higher—"like the Christ." Nick nodded as if to say "of course." Nadia remembered the time she'd accidentally knocked a piece of pita to the floor, how her grandmother had gasped and snatched it up and kissed it. She'd made Nadia kiss it too. After that, Nadia wondered if she had to do the same with plain old American bread. But nobody said, and she decided no.

Nick dug a bottle out of his suitcase and brought it to the table. "Please, for you." He handed it to Nadia's father.

"'*Araq?*"

"We call *ouzo*. It is the exact same."

Juice glasses came out. Nadia's grandfather poured a little in each one and added water, turning the clear liqueur a milky white. Nadia drank in the licorice smell of anisette.

Her grandmother raised her glass. *"Sahha,"* she said. "Good health to our guest."

"Drink everyone," her grandfather said. *"'Araq* it makes no headache. If try, you cannot get drunk."

Nick laughed. "That is what my father says."

By the end of the evening Nadia's grandfather was calling Nick *'ammu.*

"It means 'uncle,' " Nabil explained. "It's what he calls his friends."

On Saturday, the children came back from their sleepover at a cousin's house. At first, they were shy, but Nick pulled out his wallet and showed them a photo of Aphrodite, the pony he'd had to leave behind in Cyprus. He told stories that painted pictures. How he'd fed and groomed her from the time she was a foal and taught her to take a saddle, ridden her on dirt roads past acres of olive groves and vineyards, raced her on the wet sand along the coast. When he said his final good-bye to her, he swore she'd cried. "Real tears, like you or me."

"Miskini," the girl said, turning to her mother, "poor thing." She turned back to Nick. "Who's taking care of her now?" Nadia could see that her brother was also listening for the answer.

"My cousin and his wife and little girl. So you see she has family to talk with her and love her."

Nadia loved it that Nick said that.

In the evening they were all invited to a relative's wedding, someone Nadia had never met, but there was no staying home. The ceremony was in the Melkite church. "They do everything the same as us," her father said. "Who's us?" she thought though she knew what he meant.

With Nick on one side of her and her *sittu* on the other, Nadia watched the exchange of rings—three times they were swapped between bride and groom. Her grandmother nudged her. Nadia saw she was holding up three fingers at her waist. "Father, Son, Holy Spirit," her grandmother whispered. She brought two fingers and a thumb together—as if reaching for a pinch of salt—and crossed herself. The trinity again. When the crowns appeared, Nadia remembered photos from her parents' wedding album though she hadn't seen them since she was a little girl. She leaned forward to look down the pew at her father. He seemed to be watching to see what would happen next. As if he hadn't been through this twice himself.

Between courses at the reception, people started pushing back their chairs and getting up to dance. It was what Nadia had been dreading. She could do a kind of disco but only if there were enough company on the floor for camouflage. She hated the way nondancers looked on, snapping fingers, whispering comments.

But it wasn't that kind of wedding. It was old-country style, with dances that villagers in Lebanon had done for generations. Women took turns getting up to dance, alone or in pairs, their arms framing their faces or bent seductively behind their backs, their shoulders undulating like a river current. On the fringe of the dance floor, awkward prepubescent girls—her stepsister among them—were mimicking grown women and older sisters. Her father and his wife sat side by side, nodding at their daughter, calling out encouragement in Arabic, keeping time with their applause. Nadia saw that Nick was also clapping.

Nadia's grandfather slipped into a seat beside her and brought his mouth close to her ear. "Your mother," he said, "she used to dance like girls from home." Nadia was startled and somehow hurt. Except to ask after her in a general way, he never mentioned Dottie. To think that *Jiddu* had been carrying around that image of her all these years. And now she remembered a scene she'd long forgotten, her mother dancing barefoot in the living room, in front of Nadia and her father. She was wearing green harem pants over a black leotard, clinking finger cymbals, and beckoning to Nabil to join her. When he wouldn't budge, she'd taken Nadia firmly by the wrist and pulled her to her feet. Nadia had whirled away from her and kept whirling until she got dizzy, or pretended to, and collapsed into a chair. "Bad as your father," Dottie had said.

In syncopated rhythm, two steps forward, one step back, Nadia's *sittu* was edging onto the floor. Her ankles were heavy, and she was short of breath, but her body remembered what it was to dance. In a moment, Nadia's *jiddu* followed. Her hands cupped and beckoning, she retreated; he advanced. She turned her back and he came after, holding out his arms as if to show her off, pleading his case with every gesture until she laughed and said, *"Khalas!* Enough, old man."

And now Nadia's stepmother was on the floor, arching her back, moving in languid circles before her husband; and now she was in front of Nadia, smiling, inviting her to take her place. "In honor of the bride."

"Go ahead," Nick said. Her cheeks burning, Nadia shook her head.

Her grandfather slipped his hand around her arm. "Dance with me, my heart."

"I don't know how."

"I will teach you."

"Not now. I can't."

"*Itrikha*," her grandmother said. "Don't keep after her." She reached over and covered Nadia's hand with her own.

Nadia thought, "I will remember this moment all my life." She could not look Nick in the eye.

After the wedding cake was cut, the music began, one man strumming on the oud, another drumming on a dirbakki, the third a showman on the tambourine. Soon half the room, it seemed, was on its feet, hands linked in a dance that wove between the tables like a snake. Bodies thrown forward, then head thrown back, then forward again, a kick, another step, and stamping on the floor. As it passed their table, Nadia's sister broke out of the line, took Nick by the hand and drew him from his chair; he went willingly, laughing and dragging Nadia with him. She tried to resist, but her hand was firmly in his grasp. She knew the steps, she'd seen them done a dozen times and, as a little girl, had even practiced them at home. Nick watched the dancers' feet and soon caught on. Nadia kept her head down, afraid of making a mistake, wondering if she looked like she belonged.

Doubling in on itself, the line moved in two directions at once like a clothesline through a pulley, then straightened out, forging across the floor. Dancers in the rear struggled to keep up. Soon it changed pattern again, curling into a spiral. At the center, the leader broke free, beating a rapid tattoo with his heels, his arm raised over his head, twirling a handkerchief. An old woman stepped in, for a moment, to partner him, her hand to her mouth in a jubilant trill.

Nadia stopped thinking, her mind no longer in charge of her

limbs, her body on its own. As the musicians picked up the tempo, she felt sweat run down her back, the floor seemed to pulse under her feet. Faster and faster—people began falling out—Nadia held on, no turning back, no space for questioning. The room was a whirl, but she caught a glimpse of her *jiddu*, his arms lifted high in applause. She looked at Nick, who was looking at her, and they laughed.

Wedged between tables, then slithering free, the line coiled again and embraced her. It was dancing her home.

Dottie met them at the airport. She held out her arms to Nadia and even took in Nick with her smile.

"How was it?"

Nadia hugged her mother. "It was good."

"I'll bring the car around."

"Wait, Mom." She reached into her purse and pulled out a photo. Dottie saw the back of a man's head and, over his shoulder, a circle of dancers. At first glance, she almost missed Nadia, slightly out of focus, her hair fallen over her eyes. But there she was, dancing in sync with her mates. Leaning back, lips parted, leg raised, a link in a chain—unless you happened to love her, little to set her apart.

Dottie smiled. "Look at you."

"Mom, you can keep it. *Jiddu* said it's for you."